Ip Dip Sky Blue
Stories in and out of the playground

Eight lively and intriguing stories to dip into from
Margaret Mahy, Berlie Doherty, Martin Waddell,
John Agard, Saviour Pirotta, Jacqueline Roy, Lisa
Taylor and Mary Hoffman.

Other Young Lions Storybooks

Collected by

MARY HOFFMAN

Ip Dip Sky Blue
Stories in and out of the playground

Illustrated by David McTaggert

Young Lions
An Imprint of HarperCollinsPublishers

First published by William Collins Sons & Co. Ltd 1990
First published in Young Lions 1992

Young Lions is an imprint of
HarperCollins Children's Books,
a division of HarperCollins Publishers Ltd,
77–85 Fulham Palace Road,
Hammersmith, London W6 8JB

Printed and bound in Great Britain by
HarperCollins Manufacturing, Glasgow

CONTENTS

*To the memory of Lisa Taylor,
who was a good writer, and
would have been a great one.*

Deadly Letter
by Mary Hoffman

Prity didn't know which was the worst thing about her first day at Tollbridge Juniors, but there was plenty to choose from. For a start, there was the cold – though that wasn't really the school's fault. They hadn't turned the boiler on yet "because it's such a mild autumn", her teacher Mrs Shepherd explained. Prity shuddered. If freezing winds and damp drizzle counted as "mild", how was she going to bear the winter in this terrible country?

She thought the dinner might warm her up but she couldn't eat much of it. There were things they called samosas but she couldn't recognise the shape or the taste of them; they were dry, too, and the dinner lady served them with a dollop of mashed potato and some bright orange beans. Pudding was

7

an even drier sort of biscuit and a banana milk-shake.

Then there were all the jokes about her name. Somehow grown-ups didn't seem to be able to stop themselves from saying "What a pretty name!" before realising and getting embarrassed. After that, there was no avoiding some kids calling out things like "Pretty ugly" or "Pretty stupid" after her. Where Prity came from, her name wasn't at all unusual. She found all the tough-sounding English names like Dwayne and Brooke much stranger.

Prity knew English from her school in India; in fact, most of her lessons there had been in English. But they spoke a different English in Tottenham. When the children spoke to a teacher, they didn't say "sir" or "miss", and when they told a story they began, "There was this man, right?" and Prity didn't know who the man was supposed to be.

But really the worst part was playtime. Standing in the playground shivering in her new duffel coat and watching all the children who had known one another since they were in nursery school, Prity wondered how she was ever going to fit in. There were other Asian kids at Tollbridge of course, but most of them had been born in London and talked with Tottenham accents just like the white children. They didn't seem to mind the cold, the food, or the people. They hadn't got off a plane two weeks ago, leaving everything familiar behind them in the sun.

There was a group near Prity in the playground,

dipping out to see who was going to be "it" for a game. They had been playing for some time and using a word that Prity knew was bad but this time the duty teacher was nearby so they used the clean version:

Ip dip sky blue
Who's it, not you.
Not because you're dirty,
Not because you're clean,
My mum says you're the fairy queen.
O-U-T spells out
So out you must go.

The "it" chosen this time was Casey Gill, who was one of the four children at Prity's table in class. "Want to play?" she called out, but Prity shook her head. She wanted to work out the rules by watching first. But she hadn't understood them by the time the bell went for afternoon school and she hadn't played with anyone.

By the end of school, when she had to collect her little sister from the Infants, Prity had a splitting headache. Children were pouring out of the school and down the road and some of them were very big. A fourth-year boy, not looking where he was going, brushed past them and pushed Prity off the pavement. Tears started to her eyes and she had to blink them away.

The boy stopped and turned back. "Sorry, mate,"

he said. He was a tall well-built Asian boy with nice eyes and a big grin. He looked just like the white fourth-year boys apart from his skin. Prity shook her head and said, "It doesn't matter." The boy gave her another friendly smile and said, "See you, then" and ran off.

The next day, Prity took a packed lunch in a plastic carrier bag. She sat at a table with some girls from her class. They all had pink or red lunch boxes with My Little Pony or Wuzzles on them and matching thermos flasks filled with orange juice. Prity tried to hide the paratha and pickle that her mother had hastily wrapped up for her when she said she hadn't been able to eat the school dinner.

She had forgotten to bring anything to drink and she was very thirsty. Out in the playground in the cold again after dinner, Prity plucked up the courage to ask Casey where she could get some water.

"You should have asked the dinner ladies," Casey said. "The drinking fountain's broken."

Then, seeing how downcast Prity looked, Casey ran back in and fetched her Garfield thermos.

"There's a bit of squash left in here if you want it."

Prity gratefully drank the sweet, slightly sticky orange drink and gave the flask back to Casey.

"Coming to play Deadly Letter?" asked Casey.

So Prity tried to join in the game she had watched the day before, but she kept doing something wrong and all the other children shouted at her to stay back when she tried to step forward. In the end she dropped out and leant against the wall till the bell went, thinking of her friend Kamini in India and of how it was only three weeks since she had been playing with her in the road outside her family's house.

It had been warm there and the air was clear. In India, everything had sharp, well-defined outlines, the school building, the peepul tree in the yard, the buffalo carts in the fields. Here, everything was grey and misty and confusing. No one was exactly unfriendly and some of them, like Casey and Mrs Shepherd, were really nice, but all the same Prity went home every day with her head too full and the rest of her feeling empty.

At the weekend her aunt bought Prity a Rainbow
Brite lunch box and a pair of jeans from the market.
Her mother made her some cheese sandwiches with
white bread and wrapped them in clingfilm. Prity
didn't feel quite so different during her second week,
but she still didn't know how to play Deadly Letter.

Several times she saw the big fourth-year boy
who had knocked her off the pavement on her first
day and he always smiled at her and waved.

"I didn't know Nosher was a friend of yours,"
said Steve Duffy, who also sat at Prity's table. "He's
a hard man."

"He's probably her cousin," said Shane Romayne,
who was the fourth member of their group. "All the
Pakis in school seem to be related to each other."

He didn't say it as if he meant to be horrible but
Prity felt her cheeks go hot as she said, "He's not
my cousin and I come from India, not Pakistan."

"All right, all right, no need to get your knickers
in a twist!" said Shane.

Prity soon learnt that the children often sounded
ruder than they meant to be. A lot of them used
language that would have shocked her parents, but
Prity was beginning to get used to it. And Shane
was quite nice to her, really. Once or twice he
warned her about kids whose families didn't like
black or Asian people. He said they were racists.
They didn't try anything on Shane, who was a head
taller than any other second-year.

At half term, Prity had her hair cut. Her mother

sighed and kept the long black plait to take home and wrap in tissue paper, but Prity felt exhilarated. She could toss her hair now that it was a shiny shoulder-length bob. She was practising tossing it as she walked through the market when she bumped into Nosher, who was looking at cassettes on the cut-price stall.

"Hi," he said. Then he put out his hand and added "I'm Nosher, by the way, at least that's what everyone calls me."

Prity shook his hand awkwardly and said, "I'm Prity", cursing her slowness for not thinking of a different way to say it. But Nosher just smiled.

"Do you know what my real name is?" he asked. "Nosherwan Jassawalla. Imagine being stuck with that mouthful at Tollbridge Juniors!"

It was funny to think of Nosher having to make any effort to be accepted at school. Like all the fourth-years, he behaved as if he owned the place. But Prity was beginning to see how she might feel the same by the time she was a fourth-year.

After half term, Casey asked Prity to her birthday party. There were lots of children from their class there. It was the day before Hallowe'en, and Casey's mum had organised a disco with flashing lights. The children were all supposed to wear orange and black. Shane came carrying a bag of satsumas. "I'm black already," he said, and laughed loudly at his own joke.

Prity danced once with him and once with Steve,

but mostly she danced on her own or with other girls. She was wearing orange silk churidars with a black dupatta of her mother's. It wasn't exactly disco gear but everyone said she looked good in it.

The day after, at school, Prity felt like one of the gang, until she tried to play Deadly Letter again. Kevin Walsh was "it" and he said, "The Deadly Letter is 'I'", but when he called out "I" a few minutes later and Prity tried to step forward, he shouted at her:

"Go back to the beginning, you stupid Paki!"

Prity stepped back, feeling too numb to move away from the game and too miserably self-conscious to go on playing. Then there was a rushing sound like a whirlwind moving across the playground and suddenly Nosher was in the middle of the group. He grabbed Kevin under the arms and lifted him till the younger boy's face was level with his.

"Who are you calling names?" he hissed, and Kevin just shook his head.

"Sorry, Nosher," he whispered.

"You all hear that?" asked Nosher, looking round the group, still holding Kevin in the air. "This little nerd is very sorry. And so will the rest of you be if anyone else tries it." Then he dropped Kevin like an empty duffel bag and walked over to Prity. "Pick you up after school," he said, and it was a statement, not a question.

The bell rang and Prity had never been so glad to hear it. Her face was burning; this was the most embarrassing thing that had ever happened to her. On her way into class, Kevin whispered, "I never knew you had a minder", and during storytime Casey slipped her a note that said, "He's got dishy eyes! Lucky you." Prity wondered if there was any way she could avoid Nosher at the end of school.

But there he was talking to her little sister Romila in the Junior library where the little kids waited for their bigger brothers and sisters to take them home. The three of them set off together, Romila chattering to Nosher as if he were an old friend. At last, he gave her a stick of bubblegum, and turned to Prity.

"Thank you for what you did," she said.

"It's OK."

"Only . . . I wish you hadn't."

Nosher stopped and looked at her in amazement but Prity rushed on: "I mean, I wanted to work out how to fit in for myself and now they're saying I've got a minder or a boyfriend and stuff like that and I'll never be able to make it by myself if you try to rescue me."

There was quite a pause, then Nosher said, "You've got plenty of bottle, I'll say that for you. Some of these white kids are so ignorant – like that wally Walsh. They call us all "Paki" even though you're a Hindu and I'm a Parsee. Kids like Walsh have never been further from Tottenham than Liverpool to see Spurs play away. It's all Paki, Paki, Paki to them!"

He smacked his hand against a lamp post, he was

so angry. Romila watched him with big eyes and blew a huge sweet-smelling bubble. As she popped it, Nosher relaxed and swung her up on to his shoulders.

"So you want me to keep out of it?" he said to Prity. But he didn't sound angry any more.

"There's one thing you can do," she said. "If you know how – tell me how to play Deadly Letter!"

The rest of the way home, Nosher explained the rules to her, though he said it was a long time since he'd played it. As soon as he said that it was like "Simon Says", Prity understood what she had been getting wrong.

"You only move if you've got the letter in either of your names, unless it's the Deadly one and then you must stay still or you'll be sent back to the beginning," he said.

Within a few days, Prity was playing Deadly Letter as well as anyone. She also learned Forty Forty and Mousey-Come-Riding and lots of others. By the end of term, she couldn't remember why she had hated Tollbridge so much. Nosher hadn't walked her home again, though she often saw him in the playground or in the market on Saturdays and he still smiled and waved.

At the beginning of December, Prity got a letter from Kamini in India. It made her feel so strange and muddled that she didn't notice that her mother also had a letter, postmarked Coventry. When the girls got in from school that day, Aunty Veena was red-eyed but their mother was obviously happy.

"I have something to tell you," she said. "We are moving to Coventry. Daddy has found us a flat and we can join him in time for Christmas!"

Prity was stunned. "But what about school?" she asked.

"He has already seen the headmistress of the nearest primary school and you can both start there next term. It's all worked out very well. Isn't it wonderful?"

Prity didn't want to upset her mother, who was so excited about all the family being together again. But she felt as if she had a cold, heavy lump inside her, like a snowball she wanted to throw at someone. She would have to start all over again – new people, new games, new rules to learn. Prity felt weary at the thought.

"Can I go out for a bit, Amma?" she asked. "I want to go and tell my friend."

Her mother probably thought she meant Casey, but she was too busy to ask questions. She was already sorting out clothes, while Aunty Veena followed her round the house, giving her lots of advice to cover up how upset she was that they were going.

Prity slipped out into the street, taking deep breaths of the icy air. She knew where Nosher lived, even though she had never been inside his house. He came to the door when she knocked and was obviously surprised to see her, but asked her in. Mrs

Jassawalla made her welcome and went to make some tea.

"Come on then, tell," said Nosher when they were on their own. "It must be something important to bring you out again on a night like this." Prity nodded. The lump in her chest had been getting bigger and now she could hardly force her words out past it. "We're going away – moving to Coventry."

Nosher took her hand and the tears started to flow. "That's better," he said, giving her his not very clean hankie and letting her have her cry. When all that was left were sobs and sniffles, he said: "I won't say never mind because, knowing you, you're going to mind a lot, but you'll make a go of it. You've got the bottle for it."

Then he suddenly jumped up, as his mother brought in the tea. "That reminds me! I won't be a minute," and he rushed out of the room. Prity drank the hot sweet tea with cinnamon and cardamom and talked to Nosher's mother. He was soon back, with a paper bag in his hand. "Here," he said "I was going to give you this at Christmas, but you can have it now, just to remind you that you can make it on your own." It was a small green glass bottle.

That night, Prity lay in bed feeling exhausted. Of course she wanted to see her father again, but she had been so busy with her life at school that she hadn't really missed him these last few months. He had been working in Coventry and living in a rented

room while the rest of them stayed with Aunty
Veena. But now she wished his letter had never
come or at least hadn't come so soon. She fell asleep
and dreamed of a playground full of strangers
playing a game called "Kevin says" in which the
rules changed every time she tried to play.

The next few weeks sped by. There were all the
goodbyes at school and promises to write from
Casey and Shane. Prity thought of her letter from
Kamini, still unanswered. Christmas in their new
flat in Coventry was a bit of a shambles but they
did have a pudding and a tree, things they hadn't
been able to get in India, although they had always
celebrated Christmas as well as Diwali and Holi.

The new year came in with snow and the girls
were given leg-warmers and ear-muffs. Then came
the first day of term and Prity walked Romila to
their new school, Canning Street Primary. It was
old and red brick – just like Tollbridge – and had
the same smell of cabbage in the corridors. Prity left
Romila in the Infants with her new teacher and went
to join the second-year juniors.

"We have a new girl today," said her teacher, Mr
Brown, just as Mrs Shepherd had done a term
before. "Would you like to stand up and tell us your
name and where you come from?"

Prity stood up, her fingers curling round the little
glass bottle in her trouser pocket. In a clear voice
she said, "My name is Prity Vajir."

"That's a pretty name," said Mr Brown. Then he

stopped and blushed. A few children giggled.

"Yes it is," said Prity, "but you can see it has some disadvantages. And I am from Cawnpore in India." She sat down, her heart thudding hard, and the day's business went on.

At break time a tall red-haired girl called Lauren came over to her.

"Want to play?" she asked.

"Sure," said Prity.

"Do you know any Indian games?" asked Lauren, trying to be friendly.

"Not really," said Prity, grinning, "but I learnt a good English one in Tottenham!"

And soon all the first- and second-years in Canning Street's playground were playing Deadly Letter.

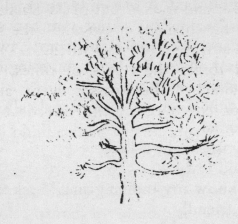

The World's Highest Tray Cloth
by Margaret Mahy

"Last day of school," said Helen, in a pleased voice. "We'll be out early."

"Don't forget to come to the Shaws after school. I'm visiting Peggy Shaw this afternoon," her mother told her. "Come back with Rona."

"Do I have to?" asked Helen in a whiny voice. "I don't like Rona, and also she's finished her tea-tray cloth."

"For goodness' sake!" her mother replied sharply. "I'd forgotten about that. It was meant to be finished by the end of term. Be sure to take it to school with you."

"Do I have to?" asked Helen again. "I'll get more marks if Mrs Sinclair doesn't see it."

But her mother got the tea-tray cloth from the

sewing drawer and took it out of its plastic bag. "It does look a bit chronic, doesn't it?" she said. "Six weeks to do two rows of cross stitch!"

"I've had to do them lots of times, though," Helen explained. "The crosses went all funny. You're supposed to count the threads but I just guess every now and then. I had to undo it, and do it over again and I got behind."

"I'll say you did," her mother said rather sarcastically. Then she added, "You could have caught up by doing some at home, of course, instead of spending every spare minute of your time up those old trees."

"But home-time's playing-time," Helen cried. "You don't want me to get ill with too much work, do you? Especially with that sewing!"

"Fat chance!" said her mother, grinning a bit.

"I'm no good at sewing," said Helen seriously, "and I am good at trees. I should stick to what I'm good at. I can get from one end of the row of trees to the other without having to come down to the ground once. And there's one branch that's hard to get to – you have to hang upside down and then hook your arm and leg right over it and wriggle . . ."

"That's all very well!" her mother said. "Sewing will be useful to you someday and tree-climbing won't. Suppose you want to make a pretty dress one day . . ."

"Yuck!" said Helen.

". . . or some blue jeans, then," her mother went

on. "Climbing trees won't help you much."

"If I was chased by a bull, it would be better to be good at climbing trees," Helen argued. She could see the bull in her mind, red-eyed and furious, charging at her in vain as she leapt into a tree, and then hung upside down, laughing, over the bull's angry horns.

"Oh Helen – for goodness' sake," her mother cried. "You're not likely to be chased by a bull . . . Well, you're to hand your sewing in anyway," she added, giving up argument and becoming bossy. "And come back to the Shaws with Rona after school."

Her mother went out of the room, but Helen stood by the window looking out at the concrete drive and the lawn and garden. Two high hedges shut the garden in at the sides and it ended with a line of trees and a brown fence. Beyond the fence was a busy road, houses, shops and a whole town. Somewhere on the other side of the fence was a winding river, somewhere was the sea. But Helen could see none of these adventurous places, even though she knew they were there. From the top branches of the tallest tree in the row she could see across many roofs to the school, she could look down into a builder's yard and watch lorries unloading timber and catch a glimpse of the river, but even the tallest tree in their garden could not make her as tall as she wanted to be.

Now, standing at the window, she looked sideways and could see a small spear of green almost like part of the hedge. But it was really the peak of the enormous pine tree standing by Ransome's dairy. No one could climb Ransome's pine tree for there were no branches close to the ground. Still, Helen liked to look at it. You could see it from school and you could see it from the Shaws, which was a waste because nobody there was interested in trees. If you climbed to the top of Ransome's tree you would be able to see everywhere all at once, as if you had become a sort of magician with the whole world for your magic crystal.

At school that day it was just as Helen had thought it would be – all right until Mrs Sinclair's handicraft class. There are lots of different sorts of handicrafts, but Mrs Sinclair had been a sewing teacher for years and she felt safest with sewing. Everyone had to sew something. Mrs Sinclair was very keen on tray cloths. She must have been to blame for hundreds and hundreds of tray cloths, done in cross stitch, running stitch, open buttonhole stitch and even herring-bone stitch. Rona Shaw's tray cloth came crisply out of its plastic bag, with the stitches even and the cream linen still clean. She had done some herring-bone stitches, and Helen, who liked the name herring-bone stitch, thought it might have been easier to do a stitch with an interesting name. Cross stitch had started to sound dull and grumbling even before she had threaded her needle.

"Helen Hay!" Mrs Sinclair cried. "This is terrible! You haven't got it right yet. Look – it goes crooked here at the very end. You just haven't been counting your threads. And how did you get it so grubby? You can't have been keeping it in its plastic bag."

"I kept it in the bag all the time," said Helen indignantly, and it was true. She did not mention, however, that she had kept several other things in the plastic bag with the sewing, including two good smooth stones, a long piece of hairy string, two safety pins and a stub of brown chalk. The chalk, which was to blame for many of the marks on Helen's tray cloth, was gone now, though the hairy string and the pins and one of the stones were safely stored in the pocket of her windcheater.

"I can't even give you a 'C' for that," declared Mrs Sinclair, and she marked down "C–"in her book, changed her mind, crossed it out and wrote down "D" instead. Helen was glad that that was over, but she made up her mind not to walk home with Rona. She could easily dodge her after school and, if she turned up at the Shaws just a little late, she might miss out on any tray cloth conversation. Thinking of a way to escape, she put her sewing back into its plastic bag, folded it in four, and scrunched it into the pocket of her windcheater.

In order to miss Rona, Helen got off to a running start down a different street from the usual one. That was how she found herself going towards Ransome's house. The big pine tree swelled up like an island rising out of a sea of roofs. It was wide as well as tall, unusual in a pine tree, and spread out big branches on either side. At the ends of the branches cones huddled like families of perching birds and its deeply wrinkled bark, grey on the surface with reddish-brown showing through from below, gave it a grandfatherly look. It was planted on the right side of Ransome's house, so as not to interfere with sunshine, or telephone lines, though its roots had crept along under the ground and were crinkling the asphalt of the footpath. Helen thought it was a tree of power.

As she wandered by, staring at it, she suddenly saw something that interested her. Barry Ransome, his little brother Cedric and another boy, Peter Becket from down the road, were leaning a ladder against the trunk of the tree. She stopped and stared.

"What are you doing?" she called.

"None of your business," Barry replied, breathless from ladder-carrying. They were going to climb the tree.

"Can I come too?" Helen asked.

Barry scarcely looked at her. "No!" he said. "This is just for us."

Helen did not argue because she had already made her own plans. She watched the boys climb up the ladder and on to the first branch of the tree. It looked big enough to dance on.

They stood there for a moment – no hands – showing off a bit – and then began to climb up to the next branch. Barry had to help Cedric, whose hands were too small to get a proper grip on the rough bark.

Helen scrambled up the bank to Ransome's lawn while the boys were busy climbing. She took her shoes off and wriggled her toes until they felt properly alive. Then she climbed up the ladder and on to the branch on the opposite side of the tree from the climbing boys. The tree felt as solid as a house. Helen looked at it curiously. At some time when the tree was small someone had cut the centre out of it. That was why it had spread out so widely. Helen began to climb.

The cracked and wrinkled bark on the trunk of the tree was difficult to get a grip on, but the branches were much smoother and not too hard on the knees. Every now and then beads of gum like jewels of gold stood out on the bark as if the tree were oozing honey. The pine-tree smell reminded Helen of holidays so that she smiled as she climbed. It was easy climbing, the branches coming one after the other like steps in a staircase and no nasty little scratchy twigs to get in the way. The little Ransome, Cedric, suddenly saw her and stopped.

"Look—" he said, "that girl's coming up." Peter and Barry stopped, too, and looked round the trunk at her.

"Go on. Get down. You're not allowed up here," Barry hissed. He was trying to speak quietly and Helen had a sudden thought.

"Are you allowed to?" she asked, and the boys were silent.

"Get down," said Barry again.

"I don't have to," Helen replied. She knew he could not make her, and that he did not want the sound of an argument to be heard up in the tree. She looked down.

"We're up quite high already," she said speaking quietly, "and there's still a long way to go."

"Come on!" said Peter. "We'll be able to see a long, long way when we get to the top."

"I don't think I'm going any further," Cedric mumbled. "I'm too little."

"I told you you were too little," Barry replied crossly. "Can you get down again?"

"I'll wait here till you come back," Cedric muttered. "I can easily hang on. Don't be too long, though," he added anxiously.

Peter and Barry climbed up on one side of the tree and Helen climbed up on the other. On Helen's side a dead branch stuck out a little way from the tree. It was quite dry, broken off long ago. The boys had a good growing branch on their side, but on Helen's side it was as if there was a step missing. She wondered if she dared to trust the dead branch, if it would take all her weight, and she kicked at it a few times to make sure. It seemed safe and she could reach the next branch up with her hands. Curling her fingers round the branch above, she stepped on to the dead one. If it broke she would be swinging by her fingers fifty metres up in the air. However, it did not break. She hauled herself up on to the next branch safely and rested a moment, feeling her heart thudding as tree-climbers' hearts sometimes do when they have just got over a risky bit.

Now she was level with Barry and Peter. The higher they climbed the thinner the branches became and the more carefully they had to plan their climbing.

"Hurry up," yelled Cedric down below.

"Shut up!" Barry replied in a sort of whispered shout.

They were nearly at the top, and suddenly the tree seemed to have changed. Where everything had been solid and steady and reliable it now seemed flimsy and unsure. Branches moved a little, bent or swayed when weight was put upon them. Barry, Peter and Helen were huddled together, for the trunk between them had grown thin and young, without the thick crinkled bark that had covered it at the beginning of their climb.

"Are there any branches on your side?" Helen asked. "Good branches, I mean."

"Nothing we can get our feet on," Barry said. "This one's too high for feet to reach, and there are no good toeholds in the trunk any more."

"Same on this side," Helen mumbled. "There isn't anything easy left."

"Let's go down," said Peter, who had been looking through the branches at the ground far below.

"We've gone high enough, and we can't get any higher." He looked rather ill, his freckles standing out more clearly than usual. Helen and Barry looked down too. Barry swallowed and licked his lips anxiously. Helen could see Cedric's round face turned up to them, the first big branches further down, and below that again she caught a glimpse of the ladder looking like a play-centre ladder made especially small for the little children to play with. It was a long way down and it seemed a pity to be so close to the top and not to get there.

"I'm going to hang upside down," she said. "Then I might be able to pull myself up on top of this branch. That's how I do it at home."

"Don't," said Peter, his freckles standing out more than ever.

Barry was silent. He looked down and licked his lips again.

Helen faced towards the trunk and locked her fingers round the overhead branch. Then she walked her feet up the trunk and quickly swung her legs up and hooked them round the branches so that she dangled below it like a little sloth. The bough moved a little, slanting itself down slightly under her weight.

Just for a moment Helen let her head hang back and she saw something she had not noticed before. At the end of the branch there was an open space in the needles of the tree and she could see the town. It was like looking down a sloping tunnel or through a telescope turned towards the earth and seeing a tiny picture perfectly clear but very far away. There was the roundabout in the centre of town and, further over, the Baptist church with the poplar beside it (tall but useless for climbing) stabbing like a dagger into a watery blue sky. There was the school beside a green handkerchief of football field and tennis court and there was a piece of the river, doodling along as if someone had scribbled through the town with silver chalk. And there was Helen's own house, its trees only a short smudgy green line, and here *she* was, hanging upside down in Ransome's pine tree, looking out from the unexplored green country to a land she knew by heart.

The upside-downness went right inside her – the upside-downness of then and now, of here and there. That very morning she had been at home looking at the top branches of Ransome's pine tree and talking about hanging upside down. Now, in the afternoon, here she was, hanging upside down in Ransome's pine tree and seeing her home far down below.

Suddenly Helen felt very strange. She felt she was going to fall through the branches of Ransome's pine and break like an egg on the grass below. She screwed up her eyes as the world of trees and houses rushed away from her in a sort of wild black dream, as she was sucked into a shaking angry darkness. But she could still feel the pine bark under her locked fingers and under the crook of her knees and she clung there, thinking fiercely about the feel of the bark beneath her skin. Then when she had that firmly fixed in her mind she began to think about the branch beneath the bark, and the tree beneath the branch, and the ground beneath the tree, and the town upon the ground, and slowly the world came back to her again, made out of her thoughts, built up piece by piece as she used to build cities out of bricks when she was very small.

Then she thought her way back into herself – hands and knees first, legs on knees and arms on hands, shoulders on arms and head between shoulders, all complete. Helen Hay, tree-climbing champion and, maybe, if she could get to the top, a sort of magician who would see everything at once and understand the world. She opened her eyes, looked up and saw that, once she was on top of this branch, she could easily get a little further and really reach the top of Ransome's pine.

Now was the time – the time to let go with one hand – one arm over, one leg over, wriggle around after them. She felt a button come off her dress but she was on top of the branch, first lying then sitting astride it, as if the tree was her wild green horse that she must ride across the world until it stood still, trembling. Now she must draw her feet up under her and stand up. The trunk was so thin she could grip it easily. And there, just above her, was a cluster of three branches sloping upwards, making a sort of crow's nest on the mast of the tree. She scrambled

into the branches and was safe for a moment, held by the tree which had first tried to throw her down and now wanted to look after her.

Helen found that her knees and hands were shaking. Her palms were sore and stained brown with pine gum. Her hair was wet round her forehead as if she had been out in a cold fog and her face was wet too. Tears rolled down her cheeks though she did not feel as if she was crying, just that her eyes were overflowing. She looked up and saw the last spire of the tree and then nothing but blue sky. She looked down. Peter and Barry were staring up at her, their faces round and still.

"Are you OK?" Barry asked. His voice sounded strange. It was as if he was asking her, "Are you a ghost?"

"Of course I'm OK," Helen answered and began to feel OK straightaway.

"Then why are you crying?" Peter asked. He sounded as if he did not believe her – did not believe *in* her – as if she might disappear.

"The wind was stinging my eyes when I was hanging upside down," Helen said.

The boys suddenly came alive again.

"Gosh!" said Peter, shaking his head. "Gosh!"

"You looked really funny," Barry told her. "Not funny to laugh at – funny as if you were going to fall."

"I'm used to climbing like that," boasted Helen. "I do it all the time at home. It's the same thing whether you're high up in the air or close to the ground."

She slowly stood up in her crow's nest to reach as high as she could reach. There were no more possible branches. She was as high as she could go. Now she could see the town on all sides and the river winding between the houses back to the hills, or out between the houses on to the sea. Helen could see in all directions at once. She had become like her dream of the morning, a wise magician who could use the world as his crystal ball, or the king of a green island floating over the roofs of cities.

Now there was nothing to do but to go down again, but Helen did not want to go down just yet. She wanted to leave a sign that she had been there.

"Carve your name," Barry suggested, waiting

patiently two branches below.

"No knife!" Helen said. "Perhaps I could write it." She unzipped her windcheater pocket and felt inside to see if she could find a piece of pencil. But there was no pencil, only the tray cloth in its plastic bag.

A little later she climbed down, sliding over the branches while Peter and Barry told her where to put her feet. The rest was easy. They reached Cedric, who looked at her in alarm.

"I thought you might fall down and knock me down too," he told her reproachfully.

"No way!" said Helen confidently and was first down the ladder and on to the ground again.

They stood there staring up into the tree. It was not quite the same tree that it had been. It had changed because now they knew some of its ways and could remember them. Now they had power over the tree.

"There's that part with the toehold in the bark," Barry said to Peter.

"You can just see that dead branch from here," Helen said to anyone who was listening but mostly to herself.

Mrs Ransome came out on to the verandah.

"What are you boys doing?" she shouted. "Who put that ladder up there?" She hurried over the lawn, her high heels sinking into the grass. "Don't you dare try climbing that tree," she cried. "Don't you dare. I'll call your father if I see you take one step up that ladder." Then she smiled at Helen.

"I sometimes wish I had girls," she said. "Boys are such a worry, the things they think up."

The children looked at each other but there was nothing they could say.

"I've got to go. I'm late," Helen said, picking up her case and her socks and shoes.

"Won't your feet get cold, Helen?" said Mrs Ransome, staring curiously at her bare feet.

"No – it's good for feet to get fresh air," Helen replied.

"See you sometime then," Barry called after her as she went away. He sounded friendly and made her feel friendly back.

Helen was late arriving at the Shaws – three-quarters of an hour late, which did not seem much to a person who had stepped out of time altogether, who had been a magician stopping clocks with a frown. But it seemed a long time to her mother.

Rona's tray cloth lay on the table being admired by the Shaws' visitors.

"Where's *your* tray cloth, Helen?" asked Mrs Shaw in a kind voice, offering cake.

"Gone," Helen said, feeling hungry for cake and taking a big piece. "Mine wasn't any use as a tray cloth so I used it for something else."

"What else could you use it for?" asked Mrs Shaw, sounding amused. "There's nothing much else you could use a tray cloth for, is there?"

But Helen's mother snapped, "Helen – look at

your hands, they're filthy."

"That's not dirt – it's pine gum," Helen said politely and her mother sighed, a cross sigh.

"Kids!" she said to Mrs Shaw, and Mrs Shaw and two other visiting women said, almost together, "I know", and sighed and shook their heads too.

"Holidays!" exclaimed Helen, going home. "These are going to be good holidays. I've had a sign that they are going to be good."

"No more school dinners for a fortnight," agreed her mother taking her hand. "A change is as good as a rest."

Helen walked on in silence. In a moment she would say to her mother, "See Ransome's pine tree? See that white flag at the very top? That's my tray cloth tied there with hairy string and pinned with two safety-pins stuck through it into the tree trunk. That's *my* tea-tray cloth with my crooked cross stitch on it blowing in the wind at the top of Ransome's pine tree, watching the town and the river and the sea, doing a *real* thing and not just sitting on a lady's tea-tray getting tea spilt on it." What would her mother say?

"How could you do anything so silly – so dangerous!" . . . or . . . "I didn't buy you that piece of linen to make a flag for Ransome's pine tree."

Perhaps she wouldn't tell her mother yet, because it was sometimes hard to explain what you could see so clearly in your own mind – that a flag was a better thing than a tray cloth any day – and also because she wanted to have a little time to herself with the memory of hanging upside down, of losing the world and of making it all come together again.

All through the holidays, when the wind blew in from the sea, Helen's flag – the highest tray cloth in the world – flickered, reflecting the sun like a little light at the top of Ransome's pine. Then one stormy night it blew away. But it did not matter, because by then Helen had worked out that the world was full of tall trees and that she was the one who was going to hang flags on top of them all.

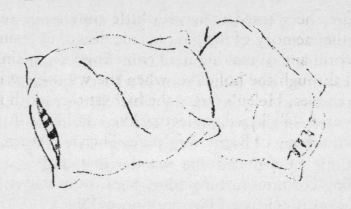

The Tough Guys
by Martin Waddell

We are the Peg Men, and we are the toughest kids at Mill Road Primary School.

We let everybody know that we are tough. We put PEG MEN RULE OK on the shelters down on the promenade and BEWARE OF THE PEG MEN on the bike shed and THIS IS PEGLAND on the toilets and KEEP OUT BY ORDER OF THE PEG MEN on Logan's wall, and everybody is scared of us.

Henry Peg is the leader of the Peg Men, and what he says goes. I'm Sam Ball, and I'm a Peg Man and so is my brother Leo. The other Peg Man is Henry's little brother Philip. Mrs Peg calls him Philip but we all call him Piglet, because he squeaks like one. There aren't any other boys down Keel Point Lane, so there aren't any other Peg Men. Henry Peg won't

let girls in it, because he says girls are soppy, even
Rosie Mitten.

We didn't know about Rosie Mitten until the
afternoon of the Keel Point Harbour Sports Day.
All the big kids from up the Main Street came, and
they were in the swimming and the diving and the
Pull-the-Punt. Henry Peg's sister Lily Peg was
Harbour Queen and she wandered round in her
bathing costume turning blue, because it was cold.
It always is cold, on Harbour Sports Day.

We weren't in the swimming or the diving or
things like that, because we are not allowed out of
our depth, but we entered almost everything else.

We were in the Sack Race and the Three Legger
and the Egg-and-Spoon and the Trampoline Cham-
pionship. I won that because I am good at bouncing.

It was my mum who spotted Rosie Mitten in her
soppy yellow dress, with her soppy glasses and her
soppy plaits. My mum went over to Rosie and said
how nice it was to see a new face at Keel Point and
how she really mustn't miss out on all the fun
because she didn't know anyone, and wouldn't she
like to join in the pillow fight?

Any sensible girl would have said "No" because
girls get bashed in pillow fights, but Rosie Mitten
said "Yes", and she thanked my mum very much
for asking her. My mum told Mrs Peg what a nice
polite little girl Rosie Mitten was.

"I'm not fighting *girls*!" Henry Peg said.

"Yes you are, if the draw works out that way!"

said Mrs Peg.

We do the pillow fight on a greasy pole, stuck out over the water. My dad and Henry Peg's dad and the harbour master and Mr Watts from our school got the pole fixed in position on the pier with ropes holding it between the harbour rail and a bollard. Then I got on the pole with Henry Peg and Leo with gooey handfuls of grease and we greased it right up to the end so that it was dead slippery, and then we shoved each other in.

SPLASH!

SPLASH!

SPLOSH!

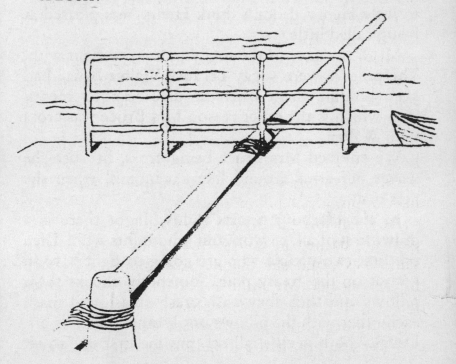

The splosh was Henry Peg, who was showing off because he can do twenty strokes. He didn't have to swim twenty strokes, because it was only up to his belly button, but he wanted to show off anyway. He put his hands on the bottom and kicked his feet and pretended to swim lots of strokes so that all the grown ups would think he was a real channel swimmer.

Walter Bruce dive-bombed him, and all Walter's mates cheered. They are from the estate at Big Road. They call themselves the Big Road Eagles and they are our Deadly Enemies. Walter's mum was mad with him and said not to dare do such a thing again to little Henry. I don't think Henry was pleased at being called little.

Mr Watts gave us the soggy pillows to fight with. The pillows were soggy because Walter Bruce had been holding them when he dive-bombed Henry Peg, which is the other reason Mrs Bruce was cross with Walter.

We enjoyed Mrs Bruce being cross, because she waves her arms around like a windmill when she gets mad.

In the Harbour Sports Pillow Fight there is a draw, first of all, to work out who fights who. Then the first two people who are going to fight have to go out on the greasy pole. Somebody chucks them pillows and then they bash crash smash and mash each other with the pillows until somebody falls off. Usually both people fall off, but the first one to hit the water is the loser and the winner goes into the next round.

Henry Peg's sister Lily was the Harbour Queen so they brought her in off her Harbour Queen float to make the draw. They gave her a coat to wear because she was shivery. Then she had to stand up on a wall and pick names out of a blue plastic bucket. The harbour master wrote them up on Mr Watts's old blackboard.

H. PEG v T. SMALL
R. MITTEN v P. PEG
S. BALL v H. ABBOTT
L. BALL v G. DODD
W. BRUCE v B. WONG

"It's a fix!" Henry Peg said. "That Rosie Mitten got Piglet because he's the smallest one, and she's a girl!"

"Piglet will smash her!" said Leo.

We all thought that Piglet *might*, so long as he didn't fall off the pole first, before the smashing even began. Piglet is small, but he is a Peg Man, and Peg Men are tough!

The rest of the draw was Peg Men against Big Road Eagles, except for Wongy fighting Walter Bruce which was two Eagles against each other. We hoped Wongy would clout Walter, because otherwise we didn't know who was going to stop him. We don't reckon it is fair Walter being in the Eagles, because he is bigger than almost anybody. We were all on Wongy's side, even though he is an Eagle.

The first fight was H. Peg against T. Small, Peg Men versus Eagles. Henry got his pillow and went out on the pole and absolutely bashed Tom Small till Tom fell in. We all cheered because our side had won!

Then it was Piglet against Rosie Mitten.

"Go on, Piglet!" we shouted. "Bash her!"

"Give her a bath!" shouted Henry Peg. He didn't shout very loudly in case his mother heard him. She was busy giving beef tea to the shivery Harbour Queen at the time, so she missed it.

Henry Peg went up to Rosie and told her the water was full of gi-normous crabs and she'd better keep her soppy glasses on so that she could look out for them.

Rosie didn't say a thing.

She took her glasses off and put them on the towel my mum had lent her, for drying off after Piglet knocked her into the drink!

That is what we hoped would happen. Soppy Rosie would go KER-SPLOSH! and come up crying!

Piglet put on his fighting face and edged his way

along the pole. He was first out. Rosie Mitten
waited. She had on a sissy swimming suit with roses
on it, just like her name.

Piglet got out to the end of the pole, and settled
himself on the greasy bit. He gave us the thumbs
up, and nearly fell off!

Rosie Mitten climbed on to the pole.

"Ready?" Mr Watts shouted. "Give them the
pillows."

It was Walter Bruce who was in charge of pillow
chucking. He lobbed Rosie's at her, and Rosie
caught it, but when he went to give Piglet *his* pillow,
Walter really chucked it hard.

SMACK!

The wet pillow caught Piglet right in the chops.

"Woooooooo!" went Piglet, and he wobbled on the greasy pole and started to slip round, and the next moment . . .

SPLOSH!

All the Eagles cheered!

Piglet went right under, and when he got his head above the water he didn't even squeak. He just sat there with the water up to his pig-snout, gulping.

"Doesn't count!" said Mr Watts firmly, and he hauled Piglet out of the water, but there was no way Piglet was going out on the pole again.

"Don't make him or he'll cry!" Lily Peg told her mother, and Mrs Peg got hold of Piglet and wrapped him up in Lily's Harbour Queen towel before he could start howling.

"What about me?" Rosie said, climbing back on to the pier.

"You get a walk-over, dear," said Mr Watts.

"More like a drop-under!" said Tom Small, and all the Eagles started grinning, and making jokes about Peg Men being cry-babies.

Mr Watts took the pillows off Walter after that, but it was too late. It was me next, for the Glory of the Pig Men.

Hugh Abbott, the Big Road Eagle I was fighting, is *very* big. He is as big as Walter Bruce, almost, although he still has a year to go before he goes up to Scouts.

I got him one BIFF – a brilliant Sam Ball Buster Bang!

It was a really good one, and he started to wobble, and I swung again, to give him my Abbott Crusher Pillow Bash, only he cheated. He caught my pillow, and pulled me towards him.

Then . . .

BIFF!

BASH!

BIFF-BIFF-BIFF!

BUFF!

I went over, but I caught his leg on the way down and he came ker-splosh after me in the biggest ever water bomb at the Harbour Sports.

I lost, because Mr Watts said I hit the water first. Mr Watts said I was cheating because I grabbed him when I was going down.

"Hugh grabbed my pillow first!" I told him.

"Pillow grabbing is in, but leg grabbing is definitely out!" said Mr Watts.

We'd lost two Peg Men, and the pillow fight had only just started!

It got worse.

G. Dodd absolutely blasted my brother Leo in the next fight.

Ker-splosh!

Another Peg Man out!

The Big Road Eagles got three men into the semi-finals when Walter Bruce KER-SPLOSHED Wongy, although it didn't make much difference, because they were both in the Eagles.

The qualifiers for the semi-finals were H. Peg, R.

Mitten, H. Abbott, G. Dodd and W. Bruce.

"Yah!" shouted Tom Small. "*Three* Eagles versus *two* Peg Men! Now we'll see who is the toughest."

It was *three* against *one*, because Rosie Mitten wasn't a Peg Man, but we didn't tell him.

Shivery Lily Peg made the draw for the semi-finals.

```
H. PEG v G. DODD
M. BRUCE v H. ABBOTT
R. MITTEN – bye
```

It was another fix. We reckoned Lily had pulled a fast one because Rosie Mitten was a girl. First she got Piglet, who was small, and now she'd got a bye in the semi-finals.

"She'll go straight through to the final without fighting at all!" Hugh Abbott shouted.

"No she won't," said Mr Watts. "She'll fight a final eliminator against one of the winners, and the winner of that will fight the other one in the final."

"It will be all Eagles!" said Walter Bruce, flexing his muscles and trying to look like Superman.

"Oh no it won't!" said Henry Peg.

And WHAM! BAM! BOSH!

KER-SPLOSH!

Henry proved it.

G. Dodd was absolutely dumped into the water, and Henry Peg was the winner. All the Peg Men cheered like mad until our mums told us to shut up.

Mr Watts said he would stop the pillow fight if we kept making a racket. So we shut up and watched Walter Bruce ker-sploshing H. Abbott, which he did with one Monster Walter Blow.

Down went H. Abbott into the drink.

"Toss up for the final eliminator!" said Mr Watts, and Lily Peg had to unwrap herself from her mum's coat, put down her mug of beef tea and do the toss.

Henry Peg lost.

"I don't want to fight a soppy girl!" Henry said, going red.

"Yah! Scared!" said Walter Bruce.

Rosie Mitten didn't say a thing. She took off her glasses again, and put them on the towel. It was for drying her when she got knocked in the water, although she hadn't been knocked in yet. She got on the pole first this time, and worked her way out along it. She was good at it, for a girl.

Henry Peg got on, and they got their pillows.

"Do her with one blow, Henry!" Leo shouted.

"Yeah!" said Henry.

"Bash her in the drink!" I said.

"Ready?" said Mr Watts.

Henry nodded, and Rosie bent forward, as if she was saying something to Henry, although we couldn't hear it. Henry says it was "Pudding Face" she said. It got him really mad.

"Steady!" said Mr Watts.

"Knock her block off, Henry!" Leo shouted. "One blow!"

"GO!" shouted Mr Watts.

Rosie Mitten stuck her tongue out at Henry.

That made Henry even MADDER. He wanted to knock her head off with one big big blow, so he let fly.

Rosie Mitten ducked.

Henry missed.

When Rosie ducked, Henry's pillow went over her head, and Henry didn't let go. The pillow swung over Rosie Mitten, and away from the pole, and Henry started going after it, off balance.

Then

BIFF-BANG-SMASH-WALLOP

Rosie Mitten let Henry have it. She hit him really hard, for a girl.

KER-SPLOSH!

Henry Peg went into the water, and all the Eagles cheered like mad. They started dancing and yelling and calling Henry Peg names because he had let a girl beat him.

We didn't say anything. We reckoned Rosie Mitten didn't fight fair, because she ducked.

"Hard luck, Henry," I said to drippy Henry Peg, as he climbed out.

"I'll fix her later!" Henry said. He was blue with cold, and cross. He wouldn't have lost if he hadn't been cold and slippy, and trying to knock her off

with one blow.

Rosie Mitten sat there on the greasy pole, grinning at us.

"I bet Walter kills her!" Leo muttered.

Mr Bruce gave Walter his pillow, and they were all set for the Final Fight.

"Ready?" Mr Watts said.

"The Eagles are going to win it!" I said. It was really naff!

"Steady?" said Mr Watts.

"Oh look!" said Rosie, pointing down. "Jelly-fish!"

Walter looked down at where she was pointing.

"GO!" shouted Mr Watts.

And . . .

BOFFFFFFFFF!

Rosie swung her pillow, and caught Walter right in his big belly, while he was still wondering where the jellyfish were.

Walter was wet and cold and greasy. Rosie's big pillow-bang started him slipping, and she followed up with BIFF-BANG-BIFF-BANG and . . .

KER-SPLOSH!

Walter was in the water, gasping.

The Big Road Eagles had stopped shouting. They stared down at Walter as though they couldn't believe their eyes.

"Araaah!" Walter said. "Ugh!" His mouth was full of water.

Then Henry turned to me. "*We* won!" he said.

"Eh?" I said. "But Rosie isn't . . ."

"Peg Men for ever!" shouted Leo, and then we all started shouting: "We are the Peg Men!" until Mr Watts shut us up.

Rosie Mitten got her prize, which was a box of chocolates, and we all cheered her.

The Big Road Eagles looked green.

"She didn't beat me fair!" Walter Bruce muttered. "It was a trick."

"Buzz off, Walter. You can't take it. Just 'cause she's a girl," Leo said.

I thought Walter was going to knock Leo's head off, but he didn't because Mr Watts was looking. He glared at Leo, and went off.

Henry Peg went up to Rosie.

"I ought to bash you," he said.

"Don't be so stupid!" Rosie Mitten said.

She thought she was all right, because the grown ups were still there, but they weren't. They'd all gone off to unfreeze Lily Peg in the Club House, Mr Watts included.

"Who are you calling stupid?" Henry said.

"You," said Rosie.

"Right!" yelled Henry. "That's it, then!" And he charged at Rosie Mitten to get his own back for being dumped in the drink.

I don't know exactly what Rosie did. She kind of grabbed his arm, and flipped him like a coin.

Henry went up in the air, and came down on his bottom.

"Anybody else?" Rosie said, blinking at us through her glasses.

Nobody moved.

"Bashing is stupid," Rosie said.

"Stupid yourself!" Leo said, but he didn't go near her. I didn't say anything, but I stayed well out of her reach, just in case, and Piglet hid behind me.

We came off the land end of the harbour, well away from the club house, and that's where the Big Road Eagles were waiting for us, down by the fishing nets.

"Five, four, three, two, one . . . CHARGE!" Walter shouted.

We thought we were going to get scragged, but we didn't.

We didn't, because Rosie Mitten sort of stooped, just as the Eagles came dashing at us.

One minute she bent down, just as if she was tying her shoelace, and the next she pulled at the fishing net the Eagles were rushing across. It jerked, and tangled round their feet, and suddenly the Eagles were flying all over the shop and crash-landing on their ugly mugs.

"Grab the other end, Henry!" Rosie said.

Henry and Leo got one end, and Rosie and I and Piglet got the other. The Big Road Eagles were caught in the middle. They were all tangled up.

"When I get out I'm going to bash you for sure, Rosie Mitten!" Walter shouted.

"Too bad!" said Rosie. "All right, Henry. Tow them in the tar!"

There was tar all along the wall, where the men had been fixing the nets. We dragged the net towards it.

"We'll tell!" Tom Small yelled, desperately struggling to find his feet, and only getting tangled more.

"Oh yes?" said Rosie. "Run home and tell your mum a *girl* caught you in a net, and towed you through the tar?"

"We're not telling that!" Walter Bruce said.

"Thought you wouldn't," Rosie Mitten said. "But *we* will. We'll tell every single person we meet how you got tarred. Unless you give up before you get tarred, of course."

There was a long silence.

"All right!" Walter said.

"No bashing?" Rosie Mitten said, still keeping a tight hold on the net.

"No bashing," Walter said.

"Let them go," Rosie said.

We let go of the net, and the Big Road Eagles scrambled out. They cleared off, muttering threats about how they'd get us another time, and calling us names.

"You're dead tough, Rosie Mitten!" Piglet said.

"Yeah!" said Leo.

"You can be a Peg Man, if you want to," said Henry Peg. "We don't let soppy girls in the Peg Men, but you can be an honorary one."

"No thanks," said Rosie. "I don't *like* bashing people, and I don't want to go round writing stupid things on walls."

She went off.

"It's just as well she didn't join," said Leo. "She'd only get bashed. Then she'd cry, and run home to her mum, and there'd be trouble."

"She *didn't* get bashed, though, did she?" I said.

"She didn't fight properly," Henry Peg said.

"Girls never do!" Leo said.

"She just played tricks!" said Piglet scornfully, coming out from behind me, where he'd been hiding.

We walked up the lane.

"Just the same," said Henry Peg. "I reckon we should stay out of her way for a bit, don't you?"

And we do!

Anyone for a Banana?
by John Agard

One of those grey, wet London days, when you could disappear into your coat or anorak, a girl named Shona was travelling with her dad on the Underground.

Nobody seemed to be in a talking or smiling mood, so Shona whispered to her dad, "Why is everybody so serious?"

She didn't know what it was to whisper easy. She whispered loud enough to make one man in a bowler hat look up from his newspaper.

"Must be all the tension and the cold," her dad said.

"What's tension?" Shona asked.

"Pressure," her dad said. "Big city pressure."

She saw her dad smile as he said "big city pressure", and she could tell from the look behind his silver-framed specs that he must be making up some story in his head.

Shona's dad was from the island of St Kitts in the Caribbean and he was always telling her stories. Once, when she couldn't get to sleep, he got her to count the beads in her hair. Beads like smiling seeds all over her plaited hair. "Better than counting sheep," he told her.

But right now, Shona was counting how many more stops they had left. Shona's school was near Wood Green, which was a long way on the Piccadilly Line. Her dad was taking her back to school after a visit to the dentist. There were at least another nine stops to go, and Shona wished that something interesting would brighten up the long journey.

A punk got on. At least, he looked like a punk to Shona because he had pink spiky hair and a denim jacket that said DRACULA RULES OK on it.

He sat down next to the Bowler-Hat-Man, who was still reading his newspaper.

Punk-Boy lit a cigarette, and started smoking.

Bowler-Hat-Man turned to him and said, "No smoking on the Underground, if you don't mind."

"Me mouth mightn't be allowed to smoke, but who says me ear can't?"

With that, Punk-Boy put the cigarette into his ear like a circus act, and a stream of smoke wriggled up past his spiky hair.

Shona thought he looked really funny with his

fowlcock hairstyle and the smoke coming out of his ear. But nobody laughed, and Bowler-Hat-Man said again to Punk-Boy: "Some of us care about our lungs, you know. If you must pollute the air, would you kindly go elsewhere?"

"Sorry, mate," Punk-Boy said. "Disgusting habit, I agree." He stubbed out the cigarette on the tip of his boot and put it back in his jacket pocket.

The train came to a stop. Doors as usual sliding open. Doors as usual sliding shut. People as usual getting off. People as usual getting on.

It wasn't busy like it was in the rush hour, so at least the train wasn't packed. Shona hated it when everybody was squashed together. Maybe that's

why they called it the Tube, she thought. Like a squashy tube of toothpaste.

At the next stop, Green Park, two teenage boys got on. One was white, and he was holding a big stereo with loud music coming through.

The other was black, and he was holding a skateboard under one arm.

Stereo-Boy began to turn up the volume of his tape recorder, while his friend, Skateboard-Boy, said, "Yeah, pump up the volume, pump up the volume."

Shona had heard this song on Top of the Pops. It had a good beat.

Punk-Boy started shaking his head to the music, his spiky hair bobbing from side to side.

"Pump up the volume. Nice it up. Wicked," Skateboard-Boy said, trying to balance on his skateboard at the same time as the train was moving.

A woman looked up from her magazine and raised her eyebrows.

Bowler-Hat-Man raised his eyebrows too, then he coughed and went on reading his newspaper.

Maybe that's what music does to some grown ups, Shona thought. Some tap their feet. Some nod their chins. Some close their eyes. Some just raise their eyebrows or cough.

And that's exactly what Bowler-Hat-Man did. He coughed again and raised his eyebrows.

An old lady, sitting next to Shona's dad, kept stroking the ear of the small mousey-faced dog whimpering in her lap. "Never mind, Bessie," the old lady was saying to comfort the dog, "never mind. It's only music. It won't hurt yah."

"Call that music?" Bowler-Hat-Man said. "Sounds more like a noise-box to me. It's upset even the blooming dog."

"This ain't no noise-box." Stereo-Boy turned to Bowler-Hat-Man. "This, for your information, mate, is a Brixton Briefcase."

Skateboard-Boy burst out laughing, and Bowler-Hat-Man frowned.

"Whatever you call it, dearie," the old lady said with a thin-lip smile, "please, not so loud. Bessie appreciates her music soft."

Stereo-Boy turned down the music very very low, more out of consideration for the old lady and her dog than for anything Bowler-Hat-Man had said.

It was then they all realised that for some reason or other the train had stalled up.

The train just wasn't moving. They were neither going forward nor backward. They were stuck, yes, stuck in the Underground tunnel, and nobody could say how long they'd be like that.

Bowler-Hat-Man kept looking at his watch.

One passenger got up and walked through the connecting door into another carriage.

Shona had travelled before on trains that stopped in the middle of an Underground tunnel, but never for such a long time.

After ten minutes or so, the train was still stuck.

There wasn't anything the passengers could do but wait.

"Hope it ain't some accident causing the delay," her dad said. "You're missing enough school as it is. All we can do is wait."

But it was boring just sitting there in the stuffy-up Underground.

If Bowler-Hat-Man hadn't been such a spoilsport, Shona thought, she could have asked Stereo-Boy to put the music back on. She was sure the old lady wouldn't have minded.

Right now, Stereo-Boy was arguing with his friend Skateboard-Boy about which brand of trainers was the best. They didn't seem too bothered by the train being stalled up, though Skateboard-Boy sucked his teeth once or twice.

Shona took out a packet of bubblegum from her anorak pocket and began chewing away.

Punk-Boy put on a silly posh voice like one of those actors doing a comic impression on telly. "I say, this is a no-bubblegum-chewing carriage, I'm afraid. Kindly go elsewhere if you must pollute the air with your bubbles." He said it just the way Bowler-Hat-Man had said, "No smoking on the Underground, if you don't mind."

Bowler-Hat-Man shifted in his seat but Shona knew Punk-Boy was only joking.

The old lady stroked the ear of her small dog. "Won't be long, Bessie, won't be long," she kept telling her.

Just then, the connecting door separating their carriage from the next one was opened, and in walked a very short old man with a yellow umbrella. Yellow socks were peeping out from under his grey trousers, and a yellow handkerchief was tucking out from his grey coat pocket.

The old man sat down without a word, hands propped on the handle of the yellow umbrella, and began whistling softly to himself.

Shona thought he looked a bit spooky, in a friendly sort of way. But maybe he was just an ordinary old man who saw so much grey around him – grey clouds, grey buildings, grey coats – that he decided to bring touches of yellow into his life. He even had a yellow scarf round his neck. Next to his grey coat it took on a special sunflower brightness.

All the while he sat there, the old man kept up his soft whistling. Nobody made any comment, not even Bowler-Hat-Man.

The people round him were trying their best not to make contact with his eyes because they didn't know what the old man might get up to.

Apart from the old man's whistling, nothing was happening. It was like waiting to see the dentist.

Then Punk-Boy pointed to the bright yellow scarf, and just for fun he asked the old man which football team he supported.

"I support the joy of life, my young friend, but I don't suppose you've heard of that team." The old

man spoke in a highish sing-song sort of voice. "My name is Doctor Bananas, and I never travel in a no-laughing carriage. I whistle to meself. Don't need a ticket to whistle to yourself, do you?"

Nobody said anything.

"Heard of the monkey who went bananas in space?" the old man asked, all of a sudden. "Serves them right for putting a monkey on a spaceship. Should have asked the monkey's permission. Should have consulted old Doctor Bananas, shouldn't they? Had a go at the control panel and all, our monkey did. After all, that's what buttons are for. To be pushed. Are there any bananas on Mars, I ask you? Well, then, only God has the right to pick the bananas that grow in space. They're poisoning the fish, they're poisoning the seals, now they're after the bananas in space. Let them be. And like I always say, a banana a day keeps the doctor away . . ."

The old man spoke very quickly, as if he didn't need to pause for breath. Then he pulled out his handkerchief and shook it in the air. Out of nowhere a banana appeared in his hand, and there, back in his coat pocket, was the yellow handkerchief. It was like a magic show, and Shona was certain that this Doctor Bananas must be some kind of magician.

He peeled the banana carefully, ate it, and put the skin into his coat pocket.

"I always take my litter home with me. Do you?" he asked, suddenly turning to Bowler-Hat-Man, who looked completely caught by surprise.

"I should jolly well say I do," was all Bowler-Hat-Man said.

"And I should jolly well hope so," Doctor Bananas said, pointing his umbrella towards Bowler-Hat-Man. The way he was pointing that yellow umbrella, you'd think it was some kind of magic wand or that he was about to conduct some kind of orchestra with it.

"Well, must be on my way to visit some of the other folks stuck on a train in the middle of a tunnel, neither going forward nor backward. Neither going up nor down. Nothing to do but wait. Nothing to do but face each other. Good bananas to you, my friends. Good bananas till we meet again."

And just so, Doctor Bananas disappeared into the next carriage.

"Well, it takes all sorts to make a world," said the old lady with the dog.

"He sounded bananas to me," said Punk-Boy. "Only wish the geezer could have done some magic to get the train moving."

But Shona had her eyes on Bowler-Hat-Man, for all of a sudden he wasn't looking very well. He put one hand to his forehead as if he could feel a headache coming on. Maybe the Underground was becoming too stuffy for him, or he was tired waiting for the train to start.

"I'm beginning to feel a bit claustrophobic," said Bowler-Hat-Man, taking out a yellow handkerchief from his coat pocket and fanning away. "I must say, the lack of air is driving me absolutely bananas."

Shona offered him some bubblegum, but Bowler-Hat-Man said a polite "No thank you".

"Then would you like my dad to tell you a story?" Shona suggested. "He's good at telling scary jumbie stories."

"No thank you," Bowler-Hat-Man said again, this time with a slight suggestion of a smile. But before you could say crick-crack, Shona's dad had begun a West Indian jumbie story about a certain Jack-a-Lantern, who at nights would make people lose their way with a mysterious yellow light.

"That's awfully nice of you to tell me a story," said Bowler-Hat-Man, "but a ghost story isn't exactly what I need just now, thank you."

"Well, how about a little music?" suggested Skateboard-Boy. "Pump up the volume!"

Stereo-Boy didn't need any more prompting from Skateboard-Boy to start the music going again, and this time Bowler-Hat-Man didn't object. In fact, he turned to the old lady with the dog and said, "I see your Bessie isn't too bothered by the music now. She's even wagging her tail."

"Takes time," replied the old lady. "But I always knew my Bessie had an ear for music. You do, don't you, Bessie?"

Then Bowler-Hat-Man actually reached across and tickled Bessie behind the ears. "I don't know what's come over me," he said. "But then I never did like being enclosed. I do hope the train gets going. Besides, I'm beginning to feel a bit hungry. Haven't eaten since lunch. That reminds me, a banana a day keeps the doctor away." With that, Bowler-Hat-Man opened the briefcase on his knees. The last thing anybody expected him to produce was a huge yellow banana, but that's exactly what happened. Bowler-Hat-Man took out a big banana and started eating it as carefully as he had folded his newspaper.

"I never leave my litter lying around," he said, putting the skin back inside his briefcase.

"Anyone for a banana?" he asked, looking round the carriage, and producing yet another banana from his briefcase.

"How many bananas you got in there, mate?" asked Punk-Boy.

"You never know, my young friend, you never know. Life is full of surprises. There may even be bananas on Mars, for all we know. Don't suppose any of you would care to join me, as the monkey said when he went bananas in outer space?"

Suddenly Shona began giggling, because Bowler-Hat-Man looked so funny sitting there in his pin-striped suit carefully munching a banana, and just as carefully putting the skin back inside his briefcase.

Nobody seemed to mind any more that the train had been stuck in the tunnel for fifteen minutes, for situations like these seem to get people talking to each other.

Soon the sound of laughter flooded the train and

echoed down the tunnel.

When at last the train was on the move again, Bowler-Hat-Man was ready to get off at the next stop, King's Cross.

"Good Lord," he said suddenly. "That old man must have forgotten his umbrella." And he gave Shona a funny look, as if they were sharing a secret.

Then, with a very dignified "Good bananas to you, everybody", Bowler-Hat-Man went off into the crowd, holding in one hand his leather briefcase, and in the other a bright yellow umbrella.

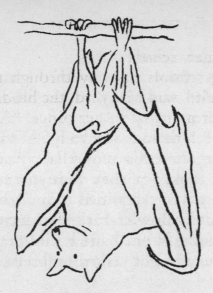

The Fly-by-Night
by Saviour Pirotta

When Biddy Beck was eight, she and her mum moved from the country to a flat in a large town. Biddy liked her new home, high up in a tower block. She loved her bedroom with its green carpet, and she liked to look down on the conker trees below.

The only thing Biddy didn't like in the new town was her new school. It was huge and dark. There was a high wall round the playground. Worst of all, the children in it looked tough and unfriendly.

"I don't like city kids," Biddy whispered to her mum as they walked through the playground and into the school to meet the headmistress.

"Oh Biddy, don't be a snob," Mum said.

But Biddy wasn't being stuck up. She was secretly

afraid of her new school mates.

"Changing schools halfway through the term is always difficult," said Mrs Bird, the headmistress, as Biddy and her mum sat in her office. "And coming from a school in the country to a big town will feel very different. I'm pleased you've chosen to come to Bell Lane Junior School, Biddy. And I'm sure Mrs Fox, your class teacher, is too. Think of all the things you can teach us about the country . . ."

"She's a keen gardener," Mum said proudly. "She used to grow sunflowers so that her parrot would have sunflower seeds. Biddy's got a parrot called Nipper."

Mrs Bird's eyes sparkled. "Really?" she said. "I'm sure none of our children have ever grown sunflowers or have such an unusual pet." She turned to Mum. "Biddy will soon find her feet," she said. "Just give her a little time."

At playtime, most of the kids in Biddy's new class, 2C, played a game called Frog in the Bog. Biddy wanted to join in but she felt too shy. She stood by the wall and pretended to count the leaves in the trees. That afternoon, another new pupil joined 2C. Mrs Bird brought him into the classroom just before afternoon playtime.

"This is Jake Wingman," she said. "Say hello, children." Some children in the class giggled and flapped their arms like wings. The boy frowned. Biddy felt sorry for him.

"Sit here, Jake," said Mrs Fox, pointing to the

chair next to Biddy.

"Hello," said Biddy kindly. "I'm new here, too."

Jake nodded. He had a pale face and his eyes were hidden behind dark-tinted, expensive looking glasses. Biddy could not tell what colour eyes he had.

During afternoon playtime, Jake stood all alone by the wall. Biddy noticed him looking up at the trees. Was he pretending to count the leaves too?

"Do you like trees?" she asked.

"Nah," said Jake.

Biddy smiled uncertainly. "What do you like, then?"

"Flying," said the boy and walked away.

Behind Biddy, a girl called Molly O'Connor started bouncing a ball on the ground. "You been talking to that Jake Wings?" she asked. She bounced her ball right up to the branches of the tree. "He's dead creepy," she went on, "so pale, and did you see his lips? They're blue."

"I don't care," said Biddy. "I think he's all right."

Back in class, Mrs Fox announced that the council was organising a competition for schools to find the most interesting small pet in the borough. "Has anyone an unusual pet we can enter for the competition?" she asked.

Molly O'Connor offered to bring her father's bulldog.

"That'll be too big," said Mrs Fox.

"I'll bring me aunt's python," said Arnold. "It's

stronger than a boa, miss."

"That's kind of you, Arnold," said Mrs Fox, "but I think we'll give your aunt's snake a miss."

No one else seemed to have an unusual pet except for Sunita, who kept a slug in her back garden.

"What about you, Biddy?" said Mrs Fox. "Mrs Bird tells me that you have a talking parrot."

Everyone turned to look at Biddy who went red in the face. She nodded shyly.

"Will you ask your mum if you can enter it for the competition?" asked Mrs Fox.

Biddy nodded again.

"Have you lost your voice, Biddy?" said Mrs Fox.

"No, miss. Sorry, miss," said Biddy.

Mrs Fox smiled. "Good. Now let's get on with our TV project."

Biddy and Jake were put into a group of children who were making a model television out of a cardboard box, some toilet roll tubes and some baking foil. Jake did not help much. He said he never watched television. He had more exciting things to do after school.

"I've got an unusual pet and all," he whispered to Biddy, "but it's a secret. If you come to tea at my house, you can see it."

"I'd like to," Biddy whispered back. She wondered what Jake's pet could be. "I'll ask my mum if I can come tomorrow."

The next day the children finished painting their

model TV and it was time to stick the baking foil on to make the screen.

"I can see my face in it," said Sunita Nanda, wiggling her nose at her reflection like a rabbit.

"I can, too," said Arnold. The rest of the group crowded round. Only Jake stayed away.

"Come and have a look," said Biddy.

"No thanks," snapped Jake.

"He's scared of his own face," Sunita giggled.

"So would I be if I was him!" said Arnold Watkins.

Mrs Fox came over. "That's enough chat," she said. "Biddy, what did your mum say about entering your parrot for the competition?"

"She said yes, miss," said Biddy shyly.

"Good," Mrs Fox smiled. "Now off you all go for dinner."

At dinner time, Biddy ate her sandwiches and crisps in the playground. Molly and Indira played hopscotch near the toilets. Jake was nowhere to be seen. When the bell went, Mrs Fox marched out to the playground, looking angry.

"What's the matter, miss?" asked Molly.

"I'll tell you in class," barked Mrs Fox.

Everyone walked down the corridor quietly. No one dared make any jokes, not even Arnold Watkins. Mrs Fox threw open the classroom door.

"It's our telly," Sunita gasped. "Someone's ripped the screen to shreds."

"Whoever it is had better own up," said Mrs Fox.

Everyone looked round, hoping to find out who the culprit was, but no one owned up. "We'll talk about this again later," Mrs Fox snapped. "Let's get on with some reading now." Biddy took out her reading book and tried to read the words but she couldn't concentrate. Who could have ripped the screen out of the telly? she wondered. Could it be Arnold Watkins? Could it be Molly O'Connor or Sunita Nanda? Maybe it was Tiffany Greg or Simon Barnes? Or maybe . . . maybe it was Jake Wingman. Biddy looked at Jake out the corner of her eyes. She was spying on him, she knew, but she couldn't help it. Stuck between his front teeth she saw something which nearly made her gasp – it was a tiny sliver of silver baking foil . . .

That day after school, Biddy's mum dropped her off at Jake's house for tea. He lived in an old house surrounded by a huge garden. Even though it was daytime, the curtains at all the windows were drawn. Biddy rang the doorbell and waited. A few minutes later Jake opened the door. "Hello," he said. "I'm glad you could come. Let's go upstairs and play computer games."

"Yes," said Biddy, "but I would like to see your unusual pet first."

"His name is Fangs," Jake said proudly. "He's a bat, and I've had him for years."

"You should have entered him for the competition," Biddy cried, watching Fangs fly round Jake's room, "he's the most unusual pet ever!"

"I'm afraid I won't be going to Bell Lane Junior any more," Jake said. "We're leaving tomorrow night. Dad's been transferred to another post."

Biddy was disappointed.

"I was hoping you'd come to my house for tea next week," Biddy said. "We could have been best friends."

Jake nodded sadly. "I was hoping we'd stay here for a long time too. But dad's in the travel business and we move about a lot."

Biddy sat on the bed and Fangs settled on the blanket next to her.

"I'm sorry about the telly," Jake said, "I know you guessed it was me."

"It's all right," Biddy shrugged.

"I can't tell you why I did it," said Jake, "but I'm really grateful you didn't let on to Mrs Fox. I'll miss having you as my friend."

Biddy felt her eyes fill with tears.

"Don't cry," Jake said. "I'll write to you and we'll share Fangs. How about that?"

"That's great," Biddy said, although she did not understand how she could share Fangs if Jake was going away.

"All you have to do," said Jake, "is say BAT, and Fangs will be with you like a shot."

The day of the unusual pets competition, Biddy was awake early. She finished her breakfast and put on her coat. Nipper was sitting on his perch, cleaning his feathers with his beak.

"Hello, Nipper," said Biddy.

"Awak," said Nipper, refusing to say hello. Biddy picked up his cage and took the lift to the ground floor. When she reached school she marched straight through the playground into her classroom.

"Is that Nipper?" Arnold Watkins asked.

"'Course it is," said Biddy, putting the cage on Mrs Fox's desk. Nipper glared at Arnold and scratched his head with his right claw. Just then Mrs Fox came in.

"Keep your coats on, everyone," she said. "The bus is here already."

Mrs Bird popped her head round the door. "Are you all ready to go?" she asked. "The bus driver is getting impatient."

Biddy picked up Nipper's cage and followed her class.

"Are you looking forward to the competition, Biddy?" asked Mrs Bird.

"Yes, miss," said Biddy.

"Good luck," Mrs Bird smiled. "We're counting on you, Biddy."

Soon the bus pulled up in front of the town hall. Mrs Fox counted all the children and told them to line up in twos. Then they entered the building and went into the hall. Biddy had never seen so many people packed on one place before. There were school uniforms of all patterns and colours.

Sunita sat next to Biddy and fed Nipper a wine gum. "Don't do that," said Biddy, "he might choke."

"Nonsense," said Sunita. "Parrots like sweets."

The competition began. A school choir sang "All things bright and beautiful" followed by a funny song called "Boomer Boomer Kangaroo". Then a group of adults walked on to the stage and sat down on straight, wooden chairs. A presenter in a blue suit introduced them as the judges.

The first competitor was called to the stage. It was a boy from Parkland Junior School. His pet was a tarantula. The judges nodded and wrote in their notebooks. Then the presenter started the clapping and the boy went back to his seat. The next competitor went up on stage.

Biddy looked down at Nipper. Sunita had fed

him another wine gum. It was stuck in his beak. "Is he all right?" Sunita asked suddenly. "He looks a big angry."

"I told you not to feed him," said Biddy crossly. Nipper tried to squawk but the gum had glued his beak shut and he looked rather sick. "Now he'll be no good in the competition. You are batty, Sunita."

Sunita looked annoyed. "Who are you calling bats?" she said angrily.

Just as the presenter began to say, "And our next competitor is Biddy Beck from Bell Lane Junior School . . ." a shadow fell across Biddy's face.

"Fangs," she gasped.

"What do you mean 'Fangs'"? asked Sunita.

Biddy pointed to the bat flitting above her head. "He's Jake's pet," she said. Fangs danced above the girls' heads and then settled on Biddy's shoulder as she stood up and made her way on to the stage.

"How do you like Bell Lane Junior School, Biddy?" asked the presenter.

"I've only been there a couple of weeks," said Biddy, "but I've made a really wonderful friend."

The presenter cleared his throat. "You're the first competitor to enter a bat in the contest," he said. "Is it a he or a she?"

"A he," said Biddy. "His name is Fangs."

"He's very impressive," said the presenter and just to show him, Fangs made figures of eight in the air. Then he settled on a string of flags and walked upside down along it. Everyone in the hall cheered.

Fangs bared his teeth and did a back flip.

"We're gonna nail 'em," Arnold Watkins shouted from his seat.

The judges scribbled furiously in their notebooks. Meanwhile Fangs did a plane dive above their heads and landed back on Biddy's shoulder. The judges laughed. The audience got to its feet and cheered. Biddy bowed and returned to her seat.

"Well done!" said Mrs Fox. "But whatever happened to the parrot?"

The rest of the competition passed quickly. It was obvious that Biddy was going to win. When the last competitor had left the stage, the judges talked to each other under their breath. Then one of them, a lady in green, stood up.

"The judges of this year's Most Unusual Small Pet in the Borough competition are very pleased with the high level of entries," she announced, "but we all agree that the winner is Biddy Beck of Bell Lane Junior School with Fangs."

The audience began clapping loudly. Mrs Fox pushed Biddy towards the stage. The presenter gave her a silver cup for the school and *A Big Book of Pets* for herself.

As 2C piled back into the bus, everyone wanted to sit next to Biddy and stroke Fangs.

"It's time he went back to Jake," said Biddy at last.

"Can't we keep him in class?" Arnold begged. Biddy shook her head. Sunita opened a window and

Fangs flew out. For a moment he fluttered at the window. Then the wind picked him up and carried him away.

"Goodbye and thank you," whispered Biddy. "Say hello to Jake, wherever he is."

The bus reached Bell Lane Junior just in time for dinner. Biddy carried Nipper's cage into 2C's classroom and put it down on Mrs Fox's desk. The wine gum had melted at last and Nipper was squawking in a very loud voice to all the children.

"I still don't understand about Jake," Biddy said to Sunita, "but I wish he was here to be my friend."

"Never mind," Sunita said, "I'll be your friend."

"Thank you," said Biddy happily.

The rest of the day passed like a dream. Biddy had to stand up in assembly and hold the cup up high for everyone to see. A photographer arrived from the local paper to take pictures of her. At four, Mum came to fetch her.

"There's a letter for you at home," she said. "The envelope has no stamp on it. It must have been delivered by hand while I was out."

Biddy found the letter on the sideboard. It was in a small envelope with curled edges. Biddy opened it carefully. The letter said:

Dear Biddy,
I'm glad Fangs helped you out during the
competition.
That's what friends are for. If you'd like to write,
my new address is:
  Flat 6, Candle Avenue,
  Mistown,
  Transylvania.

  Must fly now,
  love,

                    Jake

The Dragonosaurus
by Berlie Doherty

Joe was upset. That afternoon at school Mr King had told them that they were to start a project on pets. They could begin by telling each other about their pets, and drawing them and making models of them, and they could write up charts about the pets' behaviour, and later on they could bring them to school.

"What d'you think of that?" Mr King asked the class. He sat on the edge of his desk, stroking his long brown beard and smiling at them.

Joe ducked his head so Mr King wouldn't catch his eye. He didn't have any pets. His mother suffered from asthma, and anything furry or feathery made her eyes stream and her breath go thick and squashy. Mr King could see that Joe was upset, and when the other children in the class had started talking to each other in their little groups about their pets he came and sat on Joe's table. "Haven't you got a pet, Joe?" he asked.

Joe shook his head. "They make my mum wheezy," he explained.

"Perhaps she'd let you have a goldfish or something like that?"

Joe stared out of the window. He didn't want a goldfish, or a stick insect, or a snake, or any of the bald pets that people suggested to him. His eyes started smarting.

"I'd rather have something big," he whispered. "With a loud voice," he added, clearing his throat.

Mr King smiled. "All right," he said. "You can pretend. Pretend you've got the biggest, hairiest, noisiest pet in the class. That's fine, Joe." He moved on to Lizzie, who was already working out a breeding chart for her rabbits.

"I've only got two at the moment," she said. "But they're expecting babies any day now. If they have six babies, and five of them are girls, and they all have six babies, how many would that be?"

"Nine thousand five hundred and twenty-seven," said Joe. He sank his head down on to his desk. My pet, he thought, would be sixty foot long. With ten legs. Eleven legs. And it's green, and very hairy. And its voice sounds like metal chains jangling. And it walks like a bulldozer. Everything shakes when it walks. Schools fall over sometimes. It gobbles Lizzie up. And her rabbits. And Mr King, only I save him. It breathes out fire, and its eyes light up at night. And when there's a full moon it flies . . . right up, right over the village. Its great big shadow makes all the fields go black. You can hear its wings . . . whoosh . . . whoooosh. And when I call its name . . . Dragonosaurus . . . it comes whooshing down, getting tinier and tinier . . . and it lands on my hand, and I snuggle it into my pocket. It's a secret.

"Well, Joe, have you thought of a pet?" asked Mr King.

"No," said Joe.

Joe was the first out of school that afternoon. He put his head down and charged across the playground, making his voice rattle like metal chains. The air was so cold that his breath came out steaming like fire clouds, and his eyes stung as if they were burning with flames. He spread out his arms and flapped them till they felt like huge wings, lifting him up higher and higher over the schoolyard, over the village, over the fields . . .

"'Bye, Joe," shouted Lizzie as she ran past him. "I'm going to see if my rabbit's had her babies."

Joe gobbled her up.

He carried on flying as he ran down the main street of the village, roaring at the dogs who barked at him and at the cats who lay on their backs to have their tummies tickled. He flapped his arms at the budgie in the pub window, and as he ran out of the village and up the lane to his house he snorted fire at the steaming horses that trotted up to the hedge. He charged towards the gate to Rowley's farm and flew over it, making the earth shudder as he landed, and as he thundered like a bulldozer across the field he roared at a bellowing cow. The more she bellowed the more he roared, and because she kept on bellowing he snorted fire at her and made his eyes blaze. His rattling metal chain voice clanged louder than the cow's as he thundered past. Then he stopped.

The cow was bellowing again; long sad bellows that made her sound in pain, and her eyes were rolling. Joe was scared of cows. They were so big, with their huge swaying bellies, and their voices were so loud and dark. He tiptoed back to her.

"Don't fret," he told her. "It's not a wild dragonosaurus. It's my secret pet."

The cow lowered her head and moaned. He felt he would have liked to stroke her, if he'd dared.

Joe's house was just past the other gate at the far end of the field. When he went into the kitchen, his mother was sitting in the low chair feeding his baby sister, Louise. He liked to watch her. It made her go calm and dreamy when she had the baby snuggled up to the softness of her breast, sucking, and it made him feel calm too.

"What's this for?" He picked up a little bottle from the arm of the chair. It had warm milk in it, and a yellow rubber teat with a hole in it across the

top.

"It's a baby's feeding bottle," his mother told him. "Sometimes when mothers can't feed their babies themselves they give them milk from this bottle. I've just been finding out what Louise thinks of it. You can have a go, if you like."

She stood up so Joe could sit in the feeding chair. He sat up, proud and gentle, while his mother settled Louise in his arms. Then she cupped the bottle in her hand and nudged the baby's lips with the teat, and Louise sucked at it greedily.

"'Not bad,' says our Louise," Mum laughed. "You take it now, Joe."

Joe slid the bottle into his free hand. He bent his head down, watching the baby's mouth working, and as Louise sucked he felt his tongue pushing up against the roof of his mouth, as if he were sucking too.

"There," said Mum, pleased. "Now if ever I'm ill, or can't get back home in time, Louise can still be fed. Whatever else is happening in the world, babies must have their milk." She took the baby back and stood the half-empty bottle by the sink. "Goodness, she's going to burst with all this milk inside her," she laughed. "Now, tell me what you did at school today, Joe."

"Pets," he said, glum. "And we're going to do them all term."

"Oh dear." His mum sighed. "Did you tell Mr King that we can't have any?"

"He said I can make one up. I've got an eleven-legged hairy flying dragonosaurus."

"Lovely!" said Mum. "Now eat your tea and you can go out and play with it till your dad comes home."

After tea, Joe wandered out into the yard. He thought he might build a den for his dragonosaurus; perhaps he could prop some planks up against the wall of the garage and spread some hay under it from Mrs Rowley's cowshed. "You want to be comfortable," he whispered to it. "You don't want to stay in my pocket all the time. You'll want to stretch out."

As he was rooting round in the shed for suitable wood and making clanging noises to keep his dragonosaurus company, he heard a long lonely mooing coming from the field. He ran to the gate and peered through. He could just make out the cow, lying on its side in the middle of the field and swinging its head from side to side in a helpless sort of way. "Don't look right to me," said Joe. "Don't sound right."

He ran back past his house and further up the lane to the farmhouse. He banged on the door. "Mrs Rowley. Mrs Rowley!" he shouted. "One of your cows is badly!" Mrs Rowley didn't appear. Joe pushed open her door and shouted out her name into the quietness of her kitchen. He looked round the yard and saw that her Land Rover was missing. As he went past the barns he noticed a heap of golden spiky straw and pushed a fistful into each of his pockets for his dragonosaurus, knowing that Mrs Rowley wouldn't mind. The strange noises that the cow had been making worried him. He'd never heard anything like it before. He couldn't resist going back to the gate to have another look. The cow was very quiet now, and seemed to be lying back. "Maybe she's asleep," Joe thought.

It was beginning to grow dark now, and it was difficult to make out shapes, but it seemed to Joe that there was a lump of something by the cow's legs. He climbed over the gate and crept forward, not wanting to wake up the cow if she was sleeping at last, and then something moved and he realised what the lump was.

It was a tiny calf. Its hair was matted and wet, and it was trembling. Joe knelt down and looked with wonder at its stalky legs and its timid eyes. "Eh, arc you just born?" he asked it. "Are you all right?" But he knew just by looking at it that the calf wasn't all right, and neither was its sleeping mother. They looked as if they were just too weak to do anything. As if they were too tired to live, actually. Joe stood up and went back to the farm-house. Mrs Rowley was still missing. He had no idea what he should do.

He wandered back to his own house and crawled inside the den he'd made for his dragonosaurus. He pulled out the straw from his pockets and spread it out on the ground, then he crawled out again backwards. The den looked warm and cosy; the pale straw glinted in the growing dark. "You'll be comfortable here," he told the dragonosaurus. Then he sat with his back to the den. He felt strangely hollow inside. He knew he wasn't bothered about the dragonosaurus any more. He kept thinking about the calf's feeble efforts to lift its head up, and of the cow lying still and quiet on her side with her eyes closed. There was nobody to look after them. Except him. He ran into the house.

"Mum!" he shouted. "There's a baby calf, and it's badly."

His mother was upstairs, bathing the baby and singing to her. She called down to him to stay in because it was getting too dark to play outside.

"But the calf . . .!" he wailed.

His mother started singing again. Joe looked wildy round the kitchen for something that might help, and saw Louise's bottle, still half-full of milk. He grabbed it from the draining board and pulled her pink cuddly blanket from her pram, and ran out again to the field. It was almost too dark to see anything, but he could hear the cow's laboured breathing and the light feeble panting of the calf, and as he crept up to them he could see the gleam of their eyes as they turned their heads to look at him. The cow moaned deeply, scaring him. He knelt down by the calf and stroked it gently. It made no movement at all. The cow watched him with her big sad eyes.

"Here," said Joe. "Whatever's happening in the world, a baby must have its milk."

He held the teat of the bottle near the calf's mouth. Its big nostrils twitched slightly, but it made no movement. Very gently, and a bit scared, Joe prised open its mouth and pressed the teat through. At first nothing happened. Then he felt a kind of trembling inside the bottle, and a tug as the calf began to suck. Joe's throat felt tight. He willed the calf to take more milk, making sucking movements himself inside his mouth to encourage it. After a few more weak efforts the calf gave up. It sank its head back, exhausted. Joe felt like crying with frustration. It was so dark now that he could hardly see the calf at all. His dad would be home soon, and his mum would be looking for him to go to bed. He wanted

to stay with the calf all night, stroking it and coaxing it. He wanted it to live.

"Don't give up," he kept muttering to it. "Keep going."

But all the calf did was to give a tiny shuddering sigh, as if it was nearly too weak to breathe.

By the time his dad came to the gate looking for him, Joe was stiff with cold. "Joe, is that you?" his dad called. "What're you doing out there, this time of night?"

"There's this calf, Dad, and this cow. They're poorly."

"Bed," said his dad. "Don't you worry about them. Mrs Rowley will see to them, if they're badly."

"But she's not in her house, Dad. I couldn't find her."

"She won't be far away, Joe. She never leaves her cows for long when they're calving."

"Can I stop here, Dad, till she comes?"

"Bed!"

Joe heard his father pushing open the gate. He leant over the calf. "Get well! Get well!" he urged it. He put the teat of the bottle back into its mouth and eased a stone under it to prop it up. The milk would flow down if only the calf would suck. Then he remembered the blanket. He tucked it round the calf as if it were his own baby sister. The cow rumbled in her sleep. Joe stood up and, as quietly as he could, ran back to his father.

"How's the patient?" his mum asked him later, when he was getting into bed.

Joe felt his eyes brimming up.

"Don't fret, Joe," his mum said, seeing how upset he was. "I'll pop a note through Mrs Rowley's door, shall I? She'll know what to do."

But Joe turned away from her and curled up. "It'll be too late," he muttered.

"Hey," his mum said. "What about your dragonosaurus? You think of that."

Joe put his thumb in his mouth and stared into the darkness.

Next morning, when Joe opened the field gate on the way to school, he saw that the cow was still lying there. Mrs Rowley and the local vet were kneeling by her, deep in conversation. Joe kept his head down and crept through the field by the wall, not wanting to look at the cow. When he went through the far gate and turned round to close it, something pink caught his eye. It was Louise's blanket, dragged halfway across the field. And standing by, unsteady on its four spindly legs, was the calf. It was alive! It was alive!

Joe closed the gate quickly and rushed down to school. He felt as if he were flying, really flying. He couldn't concentrate on anything that day; all he wanted was to get back home and see if it was really true. Perhaps he'd imagined it.

At the end of the afternoon Mr King gathered the

children round him to talk about their pets, but Joe still felt as if he were far away, kneeling in the cold dark field, listening to the shuddering gasps of the sick calf.

"Who's going to speak first?" asked Mr King.

"Me!" said Lizzie. "My rabbit's had her babies! They were born last night. She had eight! And seven of them are girls, Mr King. So if they all have eight babies I'll have . . . erm . . ."

"More than you can count, by the sound of it," laughed Mr King. "Come on, Lizzie, try . . . Now, how about you, Joe?"

"One million, nine hundred and seventy," said Joe.

"Joe!"

"Sixty-six, Mr King."

"Let Lizzie do it. I mean, how about your pet?"

Joe tried to remember his dragonosaurus. "It's got eleven legs," he said.

"That's silly," Lizzie told him.

"It's green and it's hairy and it's got a loud clanging voice." Joe put his head down. It didn't sound exciting any more.

"I expect it flies, does it?" Mr King prompted him.

"That's really stupid," said Lizzie.

"And it eats rabbits," said Joe. He turned away while the others laughed, stuffing his fists into his pockets and letting them clench and unclench where no one could see them. Lizzie was right. It was a stupid pet.

"Let's hear about Tom's cats then," said Mr King kindly. He winked at Joe, but Joe didn't wink back as he usually would. He took his hand out of his pocket and opened it out. Now his dragonosaurus could fly out of the window. That was the best thing. To set it free.

When he came out of school, Mrs Rowley was driving past in her Land Rover. She pulled in by the gate.

"Want a lift up the hill, Joe?" she called.

Joe climbed in next to her. He loved the Land Rover. It smelt of manure and metal, and it rocked over the stony tracks like a boat at sea. He liked Mrs Rowley too. She ran her dairy farm on her own, and was always busy, but she always had time to talk.

"I'm glad I've seen you," she said. "I wanted to thank you. The Land Rover broke down yesterday and I was stuck miles away from home. I don't know what would have happened if you hadn't been around to look after that calf. Well, I do know, actually. She would have died."

There was a lump in Joe's throat that wouldn't go away. "She is going to be all right, then?"

"I should think so. And her mother, though she's going to need a bit of fussing for a few days."

Mrs Rowley edged the Land Rover down her track and swung it round in front of the barns. "Come and have a look at them."

She and Joe jumped down on to the muddy cobbles, and she shouted the tail-wagging farm dogs out of the way. She led Joe into a dark quiet barn that smelt of straw and dung and milk. The cow was lying in the yellow straw, muching lazily and contentedly, and sucking at her teats was her calf.

Mrs Rowley glanced down at Joe. "I think she's yours, really."

"What d'you mean, Mrs Rowley?"

"The calf." Mrs Rowley spoke in a quiet voice, so as not to startle the animals. "You saved her life, so I should say she's yours."

Joe couldn't take his eyes off the calf's spindly legs and black bony body.

"You can come here when you like, and keep an eye on her. Keep her company. And when she's old enough you can have a go at milking her. Would you like that?"

Joe nodded. The cow swayed her big head round to look at him, and bent down to nudge her calf.

"She'll probably have a calf of her own one day. I expect you could say you'd be its grandpa!"

Mrs Rowley roared with laughter at the expression on Joe's face, and then left him alone in the barn. He knelt down in the straw and watched his calf at her quiet feeding, and when at last she stretched up on her thin legs and staggered away from her mother's side he put out his hands and stroked her. Her eyes were like brown wet moons in her white face.

"Moon", he said, remembering the dark sky of last night. "I think I'll call you Moon. That's what your voice sounds like, too. Moon."

Later, Joe's mum heard someone shouting in the field, and she ran out with baby Louise in her arms to see what was happening. She stood by the gate and watched Joe as he ran round and round the field, his arms spread out wide, whooping and cheering as if his lungs would burst if he didn't let all the noise out. He could be heard in the farmhouse, and all down the lane, and his voice bounced off the hills so he could be heard down in the village too, where Mr King was tidying up his classroom for the next day, and where Lizzie was kneeling in her back yard feeding lettuce leaves to all her rabbits.

Joshua's Friend
by Jacqueline Roy

"**E**at your breakfast, Josh," his mother said.

Joshua spooned the cornflakes into his mouth, wishing they were coco pops. No one listened to what he wanted. Cornflakes, coco pops, his mother thought they were all the same. She didn't see that there were some things you liked and some you didn't. You couldn't be made to like something.

Joshua closed his eyes. Sometimes he thought about things so hard that they actually seemed to happen. He started to think of Barrow. It was a funny name, Barrow. It had just come into his head one day. So he'd shut his eyes and thought of Barrow, and this thing called Barrow had appeared in his mind. Joshua was doing it again now. "Barrow, Barrow, Barrow," he whispered, but nothing was happening yet.

"Josh?" his mother said. "What are you doing?"

"Thinking," said Joshua.

She looked at him hard. "Go and get your school-bag. You're always dreaming, boy."

Joshua got down from the table, leaving a few soggy cornflakes in the bottom of the bowl. He closed his eyes again and almost bumped into the door. "Barrow, Barrow, Barrow," he said, and this time the thing called Barrow appeared in his mind and seemed to be walking beside him. Barrow was made of vegetables and fruit. His legs were yellow bananas. His arms were celery sticks. His tummy was a pumpkin and his head was a water melon. "Barrow, Barrow, Barrow," said Josh, and Barrow smiled with teeth of water melon pips.

"We'll have to be going in a minute. You'd better hurry, Josh," said Mum.

Joshua picked up his bag and Barrow began to disappear. Joshua felt sad. He was lonely when his friend went away. Barrow never spoke, but he always smiled a lot, and once you got used to the melon-pip teeth he was very nice to look at. He was big and colourful and squishy and round. "Squishy, squishy, squishy," said Josh.

"What?" said his mother.

"Nothing," said Josh, and he went and sat in the car.

Joshua's mother was a doctor. When she was young, even younger than Josh, she'd come to

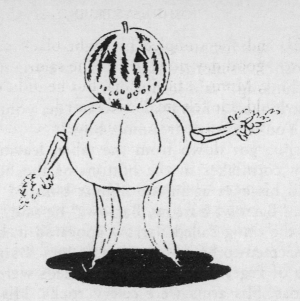

London from Jamaica. As they drove away, Josh
said, "When you were my age, Mum, did you make
things up? I don't mean telling lies, I just mean . . ."
Joshua didn't know how to explain. He looked at
her out of the corner of his eye. He was afraid that
she would tell him off or laugh at him, but she
didn't. She just said, "Sure I made up things, Josh.
Sometimes I was scared or sad or feeling lonesome.
I missed being home in Jamaica. And then I would
say to myself, 'cats and dogs, cats and dogs', three
or four times, and then a cat would appear in my
mind – or was it a dog? It was a bit of both, I think.
It had fur like a cat, all soft and black and whiskers
too. But it also had a short, stubby tail and a pointed
nose."

"A kittydog," said Joshua.

His mother laughed. "Yes, a kittydog it was," she

said, and she rumpled his tight black curls. "You have a good day now, Josh," she said.

"Yes, Mum," said Joshua, but he didn't look as if he would. He felt small and scared.

Joshua went slowly through the school gates. He didn't like school. It was a big, bad place you could easily get lost in. He didn't have any friends. He didn't know what to say to people. At school, he hardly ever said a word. He was shy, his mother said. When he went to talk to someone, it was as if his tongue got caught in his teeth. He couldn't speak. By the time he'd begun to get the words out, everyone had given up. They'd be talking about something else by then. He tried to join in, but he was always behind. He could never keep up with the quick talk of the rest. He wanted a friend, but you couldn't have a friend if you couldn't talk to people. He wished he was big and brave and knew how to handle things. He just felt little and silly and as though he were someone nobody liked much.

The bell went. Joshua had always wanted to be asked to ring the bell. It was big and heavy. He'd held it once. It had a lovely sound, like the music you hear when you hit a steel drum. Joshua walked across the playground, slowly, slowly, slowly and went into his classroom.

Joshua quite liked lessons. He was good at spelling and reading and he could do hard sums. He was the best in the whole class at writing stories. Mrs Bernard put "very good" in his book before break.

She said, "You've got a lot of imagination, Josh. It's a pity you won't talk more in class."

Josh tried not to look pleased, but he couldn't help it. Perhaps he wasn't so silly after all.

At playtime, Joshua stood in the corner by the classroom step and watched the others play. A ball bounced towards him. He went to pick it up and throw it back but someone else got there first. It was always like that. He was too slow. He looked up and saw a girl he'd never seen before. She was big, very big, the biggest girl in the school, perhaps. She had short fair hair, and you'd never have known she was a girl except for her blue skirt. Joshua started to walk towards her. She was different from the others. Joshua wanted to find out about her. He stood on the edge of the group of boys and girls who were starting to ask her questions.

"She's new," said someone. "She's only just come."

"What's her name?" asked someone else.

"Danny," she said, answering for herself.

"That's a boy's name."

"I like boys' names," she answered.

"Dan, Dan the dirty old man," said one. The rest picked it up. "Dan, Dan, the dirty old man," they shouted, all except for Joshua. He was silent as usual. "Dan, Dan the dirty old man, washed his face in a frying pan."

Danny just laughed. She'd heard that one before.

"Desperate Dan!" cried one of the boys. Joshua

106

looked at Danny, wondering how she'd take it.

"At least it's a new one," she said, and she looked almost pleased.

Joshua was still standing on the edge of the group, still not joining in. Danny suddenly seemed to notice him and she gave him a little smile, but Joshua looked down, feeling shy.

"Desperate Dan," said a girl, "do you like cow pie? Cow pie, cow pat pie, she eats cow pat pie."

"I don't," said Danny, but she wasn't upset at being teased. "I'll be 'it'," she said suddenly. "You've all got to run away and I'll chase you."

Joshua went back to his corner and stood against the wall. He wasn't running anywhere. He wasn't fast enough.

"All right," said one of the boys. "We'll all run away then if you catch someone, it's their turn to be 'it'."

"No," said Danny. "If I catch you, you have to stand in the corner. Then the next person, and the next person. When you're all caught, I'll chase you all over again."

The other children looked at each other. "We don't play it like that," they said.

"You do now," said Danny in a very loud voice. They all looked a little afraid. "Go on then, run!" All the children started running, except for Joshua, who stood in his corner and watched.

Danny was a great runner. She caught everyone so quickly that the game got boring. Soon they were all standing in the corner right beside Joshua. Nobody liked hanging about in the playground in the cold wind with nothing to do.

Every day from then on, Danny wanted to play her own special game of "it". When the others said they didn't want to play, she chased them and caught them anyway. Danny became the most frightening person in the whole school because she could make the other children do things they didn't really want to do. Only Joshua wasn't afraid. He knew he ought to be scared of her but he wasn't. In a way they were very alike, he often thought. They were different from the others and nobody liked them much.

Danny had been put in Joshua's class. She could spell and write stories as well as he could but he didn't mind. He never spoke to her because he hardly ever spoke to anyone at school. He often wanted to talk to her, though. Sometimes he thought hard about what he would say to Danny if he could make the words come out. He would tell her he wanted to be her friend. He would tell her he wasn't afraid of her. He would tell her about Barrow.

One afternoon, as Joshua's mother was driving him home from school, she said, "You don't seem to mind school so much now, Josh."

"I always liked lessons," he answered.

"Have you got a friend, Josh? Is that why you like it better?" asked his mother.

Joshua thought about it for a moment. "I might

have," he said and he smiled.

His mother stopped the car. She rumpled his tight black curls. "That's great, Josh. I know you get lonely sometimes. You'll grow out of it though, you'll see. When you get older, you'll be fine."

Joshua thought it would be very good to be older. Older people watched television till twelve o'clock at night, even on schooldays. They had as much chocolate as they wanted and nobody ever told them off. They could drive cars and go to McDonald's for tea. They ate coco pops and never had cornflakes for breakfast. They knew lots of long words and everybody liked them.

The next day at half past three, when it was time to go home, Joshua's mother wasn't there to meet him. Joshua didn't mind about this. Sometimes she had to stay late at the clinic where she worked because somebody needed her. Joshua was used to it now. It had happened before. He just sat on the classroom step and waited.

Soon, most people had gone home. The cleaners were starting to come. Mrs Bernard came and said, "Still here, Josh? If your mother doesn't come soon, knock on the staff room door and you can wait with me."

Joshua nodded, but he wanted to wait on the classroom step. It was warm there. The sun shone right on it in the afternoon. It made you feel glowing and warm and cosy inside. It was one of his favourite places. He picked up a leaf and felt its edges. It was big and floppy like a hand. It seemed to have fat fingers.

"That's a horse chestnut leaf, Josh," said Mrs Bernard.

He nodded.

"Don't forget. Come to the staff room if your mother doesn't get here soon." She walked towards the other building. She had a hurrying sort of walk, a cross between marching and jogging. Her long hair swished to and fro.

Joshua picked up the leaf again. The stem was hard. Suddenly he felt cold. The sun had gone. He looked up. Danny was standing over him, making a shadow fall.

"Hello, Josh," she said.

It was funny. Her voice wasn't loud now, it was quiet and kind. "Hello, Danny," said Joshua, except that he didn't say it out loud, he only said it in his mind. His teeth were getting in the way again. His tongue was caught in them.

"I don't like this place," said Danny.

Joshua shook his head slowly.

"I didn't want to come, you know," said Danny, "but my dad got a job down here so we had to."

Joshua nodded.

"I like you," said Danny. "You don't talk all the time like the others. You're like me."

Joshua looked surprised. "Will you be my friend?" he said, but only in his mind. No sound came out.

Danny picked up the chestnut leaf. "I'm not like the others, I'm different."

Joshua nodded.

"I'm not being big-headed. I just mean I've got a mind of my own. I don't like doing things just because everybody else does them. I like being me."

Joshua nodded again.

"I chase them because they're so silly," said Danny. "I go towards them and they start running. I mean, it's silly, isn't it? If they just stood still, like you do, I couldn't chase them, could I? They don't seem to have thought of that. They just start running away as soon as they see me coming. Silly things." Danny began to laugh.

Joshua smiled. Two big dimples came into his black cheeks. "I'm not afraid of you," he wanted to say, but the words didn't come out.

"I bet you do special things that nobody else knows about," said Danny.

Joshua just looked at her.

"I bet you think of things so hard that they almost seem to happen. I bet you have pictures in your mind that are so big and so bright that they're almost like real people."

Joshua nodded slowly.

"Well, so do I," said Danny. "When I'm by myself, I just say Puddleduck two or three times and this big, bright purple bird appears, all feathery with wings the size of . . ." Danny broke off, unable to describe them. "Well, very, very big," she said.

"But it doesn't hurt you. It's kind. It's like having a friend."

Joshua nodded a quick, sharp nod.

"I like you, Josh," said Danny. "You understand things."

Joshua looked up. He could see his mother's yellow car in the distance. He got to his feet.

Danny caught his hand. "Will you be my friend?" she said quietly.

"Yes," said Joshua, his tongue suddenly free. "Barrow, Barrow, Barrow."

Danny looked at him. She knew what he meant. "You're making a barrow man in your mind," she said. "I can almost see him now. He's got yellow banana legs and celery sticks for arms."

Joshua began to laugh. "And his tummy's a pumpkin and his head's a water melon."

"And his teeth are melon pips!" they said, both at once. They were each laughing now. Joshua laughed so hard that his tummy ached with laughing. Danny laughed so hard her face grew red and tears came to her eyes.

And Joshua knew that Danny was his friend, his very special friend and he wasn't alone any more. The barrow man began to disappear, but Joshua didn't mind that he was going now. "Come on, Danny," he said, "my mum's here. I'll race you to the car." He took Danny's hand again and they started to run together, shouting and laughing as if they would never stop.

Same Difference
by Lisa Taylor

Ask me my name. Go on! Or do you know that one? You're supposed to say: "What's your name?"

And then I say: "Haven't got a name. Only got a number!" I used to do that all the time. I didn't want people to know, you see. Stupid, really. They always find out in the end. So now I just tell them straight out. My name's Deirdre!

All right. Don't laugh. I can't help it. Anyway, it's unusual. That's what my dad says. He's right, as well. I don't know anyone else called Deirdre. Not surprising, really. I think it's horrible. It sounds like Dreary. Dreary Deirdre! But it's the only unusual thing about me. My name. Oh! And my feet which my mum says are "unusually" large. But they're not the kind of things you want to boast about, are they? The fact that you've got a name that nobody else would want! Or the fact that your feet are bigger than everybody else's! I can just imagine it – listening to Davinia in our class, when she goes on about how long it takes for her hair to dry (she's got red wavy hair which she can tuck into her knickers). What am I supposed to say?

"Well, actually, it takes quite a long time for me to dry my feet!"

It just isn't the same somehow.

Take my best friend, for instance. He's called Obi. Obiomma Nwaogwugwu. "Nwa" means "son of". So his name means "son of Ogwugwu". His family comes from Nigeria in West Africa. Obi says that if you imagine the whole of Africa is like a human skull sideways on, then his family comes from the bit where the ear would be. I reckon that's why Obi's hearing is so good. He can hear anything. You know that rhyme, the one you say if you see an ambulance:

> Touch collar
> Never swallow
> Never get the fever.
> Touch your nose
> Touch your toes
> Never go in one of those.

Well, Obi always manages to say it about two minutes before everyone else – as soon as he hears the ambulance's siren. He's dead useful if we're mucking about in the classroom, because he can warn us when a teacher's on the loose.

Most of Obi's family live over here now, but he's still got some grandparents in Nigeria. And two brothers in New York. All my relations live in Wandsworth. Same as me. Except for my Great Aunty Queenie, who's got a bungalow in Southend. But I hardly ever see her. Dad says she doesn't like children very much. I don't like her very much. She pinches and she's all shrivelled up like she's been left out in the sun too long.

Obi says it would be nice to have his family living close together. He says it would mean he could visit them more often. But I think he just tells me that to make me feel better. You know – when I'm going off round the block to see my Uncle Stan and he's going off to Nigeria to visit his grandparents. He can be dead bossy sometimes, though. Especially when we're in the playground. And if we're playing dares or anything, he always has to do the biggest and the best. I remember once, when his sister was ill, and we dared him to borrow her uniform and try to get into the Brownies. He did it, as well! I couldn't believe it. He looked so terrible. And he put on this little squeaky voice like he'd just sat down on a drawing pin. But Brown Owl didn't seem to notice. In fact, she kept trying to get him to sit on her lap because she thought he was really shy. But he never boasted about it, after. Not like

Davinia and her blinking hair. I mean, he never talks much about himself. He's more interested in other people and what they're doing. And he always listens to me when I get fed up. Sometimes I wonder why he likes me. I asked him once. He said it was because I made him laugh.

Mind you, Obi can be dead proud, sometimes. If he thinks he's been treated unfairly, that is. He says it's because his family comes from a group of people called the Igbo. Obi says that in Nigeria the Igbo people are very fierce and noble. I remember once, when Ms Bridger had gone off sick (I'm sure it was because she'd had seconds of Gypsy Tart) and another teacher came to take us for maths. He was called Mr Baggins, like Bilbo the hobbit. Except we called him Money-Baggins and he wasn't short and hairy, he was tall and bald and he had a big posh car and a voice which sounded like he'd just pulled the plug out. Anyway, Mr Baggins sent Obi to stand in the corner for something which wasn't his fault. And he left him there for the whole lesson. Then, at the end, he said to Obi:

"Well, what do you say?"

I suppose he was expecting Obi to say "Sorry" or "Thank you" or something.

And Obi said: "Igbo ama eze."

Then Mr Baggins said: "And what's that supposed to mean?"

So Obi said: "It means 'the Igbo knows no king'."

And Mr Baggins was so shocked that he just sent

Obi back to his desk. You see, if he had been in the wrong, Obi would have apologised straight away. But he wasn't going to say sorry for something he didn't do. Anyway, Obi said that Mr Baggins should be apologising to him. He was right, as well. Just because you're an adult, it doesn't mean to say you can't make mistakes. Obi's good like that. He always thinks clearly about things. He hardly ever gets cross or shouts. That's partly what makes him so special. I mean, I know he's got really good hearing, and he does brilliant dares and he blows the best bubbles out of chewing gum, but that's not why I like him. I don't like Davinia and she's got hair which she can sit on. In fact, sometimes I wish I could sit on Davinia's hair myself. I suppose my dad's right, really. He says that the things on the outside don't matter. It's what's underneath that counts. Even so, I can't help wishing . . .

Sometimes I close my eyes and pretend that I've got special powers: like gills behind my ears so I can breathe underwater or a belly button which I can press to make me fly. I think the person I would most like to be in the world is Superman. It would be brilliant. I could carry off the canteen at school so nobody would have to eat any more of those revolting dinners. Or I could use my X-ray vision to look into my brother's safety-box and check that he hadn't nicked my marbles.

I had this really weird dream the other day. It was after I'd heard my mum talking to her mate in the kitchen. Her mate was saying that all she'd done for the last two weeks was think about walnut whips. She's pregnant, you see. And Mum says that when you're pregnant it makes you want to eat odd things. Anyway, then Mum said:

"Well, when I was pregnant with Deirdre, all I wanted to eat was fish!"

And then I had this dream. I was a sort of Spiderman character. You know – with special powers because of something which had happened to me when I was young. Except I didn't know what the special powers were. So I had to go and ask my mum's mate. Except she wasn't really my mum's mate. She was all sort of green and she was wearing a crown in the shape of a walnut whip.

Anyway, I had to line up with all these other people, who were also waiting to find out what their special powers were. And my mum's mate was pointing at them all in turn and saying things like:

"Because you were born on the return flight of Concorde, you have the power to run faster than the speed of sound . . ."

or:

"Because your sister poured a bottle of Tipp-Ex over your head, you have the power to become invisible . . ." and she went on and on down the line. And I was getting really excited because they were all such brilliant things. Then finally, it came to my turn. And my mum's mate pointed at me and said:

"Because your mother ate so much fish when she was pregnant, you have the power to turn into a kipper!"

Typical, isn't it? A blinking kipper! I mean, what can a kipper do? Apart from lie on a plate? And there I was thinking I was going to save the world.

It's not that I want to be different in any big way. It's just that I'd like to have something a little bit special. Like Obi's ears. Or Davinia's hair. Davinia goes round telling everyone her hair is "titian". Like that royal woman. The Duchess of York. Whereas mine is brown. Like everybody else's. Except in the summer, when it goes the colour of manure. At least that's what my brother says. And it's not wavy either. It's dead straight, and parted in the middle so it hangs down like a couple of curtains. Mind you, I wouldn't want to *be* Davinia. Nobody seems to like her very much. And at least I've got quite a lot of friends. Obi says that I'm really popular. He said that one year I got the most Christmas cards in the whole school. I'm sure it wasn't true, though. I think he'd stuffed half of his up his jumper.

What was it my mum said? I know! She said that everyone was special in their own way. So I went through the whole of my class – just to see if she was right. And she was, as well! Even Ms Bridger can bend her thumb back so it touches her wrist. I've always wanted to be able to do that.

So then I started thinking – there must be something special about me as well. And I began to go through all the things we do at school, just to see what I was good at. Like writing, for instance. Ms Bridger is always saying how "original" my stories are. Mind you, I'm not sure what that's supposed to mean – probably just that she thinks they're a bit odd. But she always sets such boring titles. And she never gives us marks. She just scribbles stuff at the bottom, like:

"Very original, Deirdre. When I asked you to write about what you'd had for breakfast, I didn't expect a monster to hatch out of your boiled egg . . ."

And my dad's always saying what a vivid imagination I've got. I remember seeing a film about sharks and being frightened to go in the bath for a month. My brother said it was because I liked being dirty.

I've always wanted to be good at drawing. Davinia is, worst luck. She spends all her time painting pictures of princesses with long red hair. She's dead soppy. We did this project on animals last week – about where they live and why some of them could become extinct. It was called "Animals and their Natural Habitat". I remember because Davinia asked Ms Bridger if that was the same Habitat where her mum went shopping on Saturday mornings. Anyway, I was supposed to be drawing a hippo, only I couldn't remember what its feet looked like, so I ended up giving it pigs' trotters. And then Ms Bridger stuck it up on the wall! I couldn't believe it. She said it didn't matter and that it was good because it showed how much more we had to learn about

the subject. I was really embarrassed.

Obi says I'm good at acting. We did this panto-mime last Christmas. Ms Bridger wanted me to play Cinderella, but I thought it would be too boring. So I ended up as one of the ugly sisters. Obi said I was really funny. At least the bit where I tried to stuff my feet into the glass slipper must have been quite convincing. And I can remember people were laugh-ing a lot. But I think that was because Davinia got her hair wrapped round the Fairy Godmother's wand, so they had to move everywhere together. Anyway, I asked my dad afterwards if he thought I was good at acting. And he said he thought I was good at acting the fool.

I love swimming. Mum says I'm getting much better as well. I often have this dream that I'm swimming the channel and there are all these sharks behind me, so I go faster and faster until I end up doing it in record time! Dreams are nice sometimes. They let you pretend for a while. I'm not really much good at sport. Not like Obi. Although I usually beat him at table tennis. I think my favourite thing is riding. But I don't get to go that often. Blinking Davinia goes riding every week. On some horse called Snuggles. She's always going on about Snuggles. Somebody asked her once what she liked best about him – expecting her to say something soppy like: "his face because it's so cute" or "his nose because it's so cuddly" and instead she said: "his tail because it matches the colour of my hair!" She probably wouldn't ride him if it clashed.

I don't know what I'll do when I grow up. The trouble is that I'm not brilliant at anything. I'm just sort of all right. And my dad doesn't help. I mean, one minute he's saying:

"Of course you're special, Deirdre. You're very special to your mother and me," (although he never says exactly *how*) and the next minute he's saying:

"You'll go to bed at the same time as everyone else, Deirdre. What makes you so special?"

Or if I try to get out of having garbage (cabbage) at dinner-time: "You'll get what you're given, Deirdre. You're no different from anyone else!"

I want to be a writer when I'm older. Or a racing

driver. You don't have to be fit to do that. You just have to like going fast. Which I do. And not scare easily. Which I don't. Mum and Dad think I'm going to be a secretary. And Ms Bridger. They keep nagging me about how important it is to learn to type. I don't know what all the panic's about. I mean, I've got years to go before that. Anyway, I don't want to be a secretary. But knowing my luck, I'll end up doing it all the same.

No. There's nothing very unusual about me. Except for my name. Oh! And my feet! Which my mum says are "unusually" large. But I reckon that could be really useful. If I ever get out of my wheelchair, that is. I've got something called cerebral palsy, you see. Which means I can't walk very well. So big feet should be good for balancing. Not that I mind too much. About being in a wheelchair, I mean. I just want to be different, that's all.

About the Authors

JOHN AGARD was born in Guyana and came to England in 1977. He writes poetry for children and adults, which he performs in schools and at poetry festivals and on radio and television. He has written two books of poetry for children, *I Didn't Do Nuttin'* and the prize-winning *Say It Again, Granny*. He also writes stories for children. His most recent one, *Lend Me Your Wings*, was shortlisted for the 1987 Smarties Prize.

BERLIE DOHERTY has won the Carnegie Medal twice, for *Ganny Was a Buffer Girl* and *Dear Nobody* (1992). Her books *How Green You Are!*, *The Making of Fingers Finnigan* and *Children of Winter* have been read on Jackanory. *The Dragonosaurus* is based on something that really happened in the Lake District. Berlie Doherty lives in Sheffield.

MARY HOFFMAN is the author of about fifty children's books and particularly enjoys writing for and working with juniors. Her latest books are *Amazing Grace* and *The Ghost Menagerie*.

MARGARET MAHY lives and works in New Zealand, where she is a popular visitor in schools, sometimes dressed as a pirate! She often writes about pirates too, as in *The Great Piratical Rumbustification*. Her most recent novel is an exciting adventure story called *Underrunners*. Her books have won several prizes, including two Carnegie Medals.

SAVIOUR PIROTTA comes from Malta. He runs writing workshops in schools, using material from all over the world. He writes picture books for younger children, such as *Solomon's Secret*. *The Fly-by-night* was his first story for juniors, but now he has written a short novel, called *Sangarella*, for the same age group, which is also about vampires, about the search for Dracula's dentures!

JACQUELINE ROY says that all her family writes, so it was always her ambition too. She enjoys writing for all ages from six upwards, and her first novel for young adults, *Soul Daddy*, was published in 1990.

LISA TAYLOR was a talented young actress as well as a writer. She had published only two books, *All on a Winter's Day* and *Pesters of the West* before her sudden and unexpected death in 1990.

MARTIN WADDELL lives by the sea at the foot of the Mourne mountains with his wife, three children and a dog named Bessie. He writes a lot and talks a lot and enjoys visiting schools. He won the Smarties Grand Prix in 1988 with *Can't You Sleep, Little Bear?* and in 1991 with *Farmer Duck* and the 1989 Emil/Kurt Maschler Award with *The Park in the Dark*.